The Last Letter

By Scott Fields

WHITE STAR LINE

BOARDING PASS

PERMISSION GRANTED TO COME ABOARD
WHITE STAR LINE'S
R.M.S.
TITANIC

ISMAY, IMRIE & CO.,
34, LEADENHALL STREET, LONDON,
AND
10, WATER STREET, LIVERPOOL

Outer Banks Publishing Group
Raleigh/Outer Banks

Drawings of the Titanic by Norman Wilkenson

FIRST EDITION – February 2018

ISBN 13 – 978-0-9906790-7-3
ISBN 10 – 0-9906790-7-1
eISBN - 9781370958283

The Last Letter is dedicated to my grandchildren,
Bryan, Rachel, Emmy, and Addy.

OTHER WORKS BY SCOTT FIELDS

The Mansfield Killings – soon to be a major motion picture
The Killing Road – soon to be a major motion picture
Summer Heat – soon to be a major motion picture
Breakfast at the Diner – now *Summer Harvest* – soon to be
a major motion picture
Against the Wind – soon to be a major motion picture
The Geezer Bench – soon to be a major motion picture
A Killing in a Small Town
Just Believe
Last Days of Summer
The Road Back Home
Through These Eyes
Warm Winds of Autumn

 # CHAPTER ONE

The gigantic cruise liner steamed into the night at over 20 knots leaving a fluorescent wake that could be seen for miles. In its path was a two hundred-ton monster over a thousand feet tall, lurking in the darkness of the cold Atlantic waters waiting patiently for its prey.

It was twenty minutes before midnight when the iceberg tore into the side of the towering structure. Two hours later, tons of water shifted forward, and without any fanfare, the bow of the once proud ship slipped slowly beneath the water. The stern reared high into the night sky in defiance of the inevitable fate that lay in wait.

On deck, passengers searched desperately for a way to survive the nightmare that was swallowing them. Some grabbed hold of the ship's structures, others in desperation jumped over the side and into the icy water below. Below deck, water rushed down corridors flooding rooms and consuming the ship's decks one-by-one until hardened steel buckled from the weight.

Spencer Ellington ran down the hallway searching for a ladder. He had already escaped the water from the lower decks and was now on the third level. He stopped for a moment to catch his breath. Water swirled around his feet as if to warn him of impending doom. Then, the fearful sound of water flooding the hall as it claimed another level of the ship for its own.

Spencer turned the corner. At the other end of the hallway was a ladder leading to the next level. The water was waist deep and the strong current swept him off his feet carrying him swiftly down the hall towards the ladder. He leaned over and with outstretched hands he snagged one of the rungs. The force of the current nearly pulled his arms from their sockets. He pulled himself against the raging water and managed to get both feet on the ladder. The swirling water inched up his body until it had engulfed his chest and was lapping at his chin.

He struggled up the ladder until he reached the ceiling. There was a metal grate blocking his exit. He pushed on it. Nothing. He pushed again with more force. This time, it rattled. The water by now was inches from the ceiling. He cocked his head flat against the ceiling to get air. He slammed the grate with his fist and a padlock bounced into view.

The young man filled his lungs with air as the water swirled over his head and up through the grate.

+++

Spencer jumped and sat straight up in bed gasping and gulping air. He searched the room for a familiar landmark and then slowly shook his head. "Damn!" he muttered aloud.

He slowly lay back down in bed and stared at the fan hanging from the ceiling. It was shaking in a rhythmic motion and making noise. Must have been bumped or hit throwing it out of balance. Not much anyone can do for it now.

His head throbbed just above the eyes, and in a short time the throbbing turned into a sharp pain. He turned and looked at the empty bottle of Jim Beam on the desk, and was reminded of why his head hurt.

Spencer was still in his thirties, lean and tall, and with his arched eyebrows, he still had the little boy look of innocence. In school, he was voted most likely to marry the most beautiful girl in town if he ever lost the Opie Taylor look. His hair was short and well kept. He never wore a beard, yet lately, his face was covered with stained, scraggly hair.

He rolled over and sat on the edge of the bed. The empty bottle on the desk stared back at his aching eyes. That wasn't the first soldier he had killed that week. Seemed like it was becoming an everyday thing. He wondered if he was becoming an alcoholic. Couldn't be. No such thing as a thirty-five-year-old alcoholic. You had to be really old for that...at least over forty.

Spencer glanced around the room. It was a comfortable room, bed, chair and reading lamp. His older brother and sister-in-law did what they could to make it that way. Someone had to take him. He needed to somehow get his life in order and somewhere to do it.

It had been a messy divorce. Next door neighbors and childhood sweethearts, Spencer and Gina had known each other all their lives, but after eight years of marriage, it all seemed to come to an end.

Spencer had worked as a lawyer for his father's firm for the past five years. With the impending divorce, the arguments between Spencer and his father became unbearable until Spencer finally resigned.

There came a soft knocking on the door.

"Who is it?" asked Spencer, even though he knew the answer.

"It's Tyler. Can I come in?"

"Sure, just don't slam any doors."

Tyler was a big man, tall like his brother, but bulky from years of weight training. He had just been promoted to detective on the police force, a position he had wanted for most of his adult life.

How ya doing?" asked Tyler.

Spencer ran his fingers through his hair. "Just wonderful."

"Have the dream again?"

"Same one I've had every night for the last month," said Spencer. "Except this time, she wasn't in it."

Tyler turned around a wooden chair and sat down. "Did you ever see her face?"

"Never did," said Spencer." "It's always her back or side view."

Spencer grabbed a pack of Camels and shook one free.

"I've been meaning to talk to you about that," said Tyler. "Casey wanted me to ask you not to smoke in the house, something about her allergies."

Spencer threw the pack back onto the nightstand. "Need to quit anyway," he muttered.

"Maybe you need to get a new hobby," said Tyler.

"What?"

"Your obsession with the Titanic. Maybe you should find a new interest."

"Who said I'm obsessed with the Titanic?"

Tyler smirked. "Come on, brother. You've been in love with the Titanic since you were a kid."

Spencer forced a smile. "Bad enough all those people died in the first place, now I get to relive it every night."

"How are you and Gina getting along?"

"Oh, I suppose you're hoping I'll go back to her and get out of here," said Spencer. "Can't say as I blame you."

"You know you can stay here as long as you want," said Tyler. "I was just wondering."

"Actually, we get along better now than when we were married," said Spencer. "Go figure."

"Any luck finding a job?"

"I have an interview with Higgins and Dernbach this morning," said Spencer. "They're looking for fresh blood."

"I thought you were getting out of the law business."

"What would I do?" said Spencer. "All I've ever know is law. Besides, I think I'd like it down there. They handle all the big boys in town."

Tyler got to his feet and started for the door. "Well, I got to get to work. Good luck on your interview."

Spencer shaved and showered. He put on a navy, pinstriped suit with black dress shoes and a red and white tie. He was quite familiar with the interview process, both as an interviewer and an interviewee, and he knew how important a first impression was. He took one last look at himself in the mirror and walked out of the room.

Casey was an attractive woman, full-figured and robust. She was dressed in a wraparound robe tied at the waist. She was sitting at the table drinking her second cup of coffee, the morning newspaper spread out in front of her.

"Morning, Casey," said Spencer, heading for the pot of coffee.

"Well, did you see her face?" asked Casey.

"Not even a good morning, how ya doing, or go to hell?"

"Sorry, but I worry about you. You've had these dreams much too long."

Spencer poured coffee into a cup. "This time it was different. You know how I'm always chasing her down hallways filled with water? This time she wasn't even there. It was just me in that ship, drowning like a rat."

"Tyler thinks you're having the dreams because you are obsessed with the Titanic."

Spencer carried a cup of coffee to the table and sat down. "When I was a manager, I dreamed every night about being late for a meeting."

Casey picked up her coffee cup. She turned it to avoid the red lip imprints. "Maybe he's right then. You were obsessed with your job back then, maybe this is your new obsession."

Spencer sipped his coffee. "I don't know. I guess I've always been fascinated with the Titanic...read just about every book written."

"Hear you have a job interview."

"Sure do," said Spencer. "Hope to get a job soon and get out of here. I'm sure I've worn out my welcome."

Casey smiled. "Actually, it's been nice having you around. Kinda lonely during the days." She closed the paper and dropped it in the middle of the table. "How's Gina? Seen her lately?"

"Her boyfriend moved in," said Spencer. "Imagine that. He's sitting in my chair, watching my TV. Life just ain't fair."

Casey picked up her empty cup and started for the sink. "Think I have some important news for you," she said with a smile. "Read in today's paper that the Titanic Exhibit opens in Memphis today."

Stunned, Spencer turned to her. He stared in disbelief. "Show me," he said, grabbing a section of the newspaper.

Casey opened the Lifestyle Section and spread it in front of him. It's a small article, just filler for the newspaper with times and dates.

Spencer quickly scanned the article and then jumped to his feet. "I gotta go!" he said starting across the kitchen. "There's no way I'm missing this!"

"What about your job interview?"

Spencer stopped and slowly turned to Casey. "Do me a favor?"

Casey frowned. "I know, you had a death in the family, and you'll call them for another interview when you get back."

"You're a sweetheart," he said with a smile.

+++

Spencer packed a bag and was soon on the road to Memphis. It was nearly midnight when he pulled into the city limits. He stopped at a small rundown motel called The Cozy Nest Inn. A light was burning in the office, and he could see a lone figure leaning against the counter.

Spencer opened the door. "Good evening," he said. He squinted from the fluorescent light. "Any rooms left?"

An older man with dark skin and long, silver hair turned his way. "Been driving a long time?"

Spencer stretched and yawned. "Yeah, how'd you guess?"

"You look beat," he said.

He slid a blank registration form and a pencil across the counter. "Just your name and address."

Spencer picked up the pencil and began to write. "Came here for the Titanic Exhibit. Can you tell me how to find it?"

The old man smiled and pointed out the window in no particular direction. "That road out there is Fourth Street. Take it all the way downtown to Diamond Street. The big building on the corner is the Olympia. Can't miss it."

Spencer dropped the pencil and slid the form back across the counter. "Thanks, mister. I really appreciate it."

The old man slid a key to Spencer. "You come all this way just to see a bunch of junk from the bottom of the ocean?"

Spencer forced a smile. "'Fraid so."

The old man pointed. "Room twelve down at the other end."

Spencer took a hot shower and crawled into bed. He stretched out under the cool sheets and stared out the window at the passing cars. "Won't be long now," he muttered. "Just a few more hours."

They carried luggage rushing along the deck in search of their cabins. Nearly everyone was aboard now, strong men removed the boarding ramps and prepared for the departure of the Titanic, the largest structure ever made by man.

There was an excitement in the air. It was the dawn of a new age, an age of mass transportation unlike anything the world had ever known. Investors and shipbuilders alike took great interest in the launching of this ship. A successful maiden voyage would mean more ships, some perhaps larger than the Titanic.

The ship's horn bellowed once to signal departure. Hundreds of passengers leaned against the railing and waved frantically at loved ones ashore. Mooring lines were released as giant engines roared to life. All was made ready for the eminent departure of the great ship.

Spencer jockeyed for a position along the crowded dock. He scanned the decks, searching the passengers. Some were still waving goodbye while others picked up their luggage and disappeared into the crowd.

Then, it happened. There she was, gliding effortlessly through the crowd. He'd recognize her anywhere. Her long, auburn hair flowed over her shoulders and tumbled down her back. She was a lady of culture and breeding. He could tell that. Only a lady walked with such grace and beauty.

His eyes followed her as she wove her way through the crowded deck. Sunlight struck the side of her face bathing it in a soft warm glow, yet turned her hair into crimson fire. Spencer felt his heart pounding in his chest.

She walked nearly the length of the ship until she was near the bow, an area largely deserted of other passengers. She drifted to the side of the ship and leaned against the railing. She lifted her head and gazed in his direction.

Spencer froze. She was everything he thought she would be. Long, golden brown hair flowed down her face, her lips scarlet red. Her dark eyes never searched the crowd; they went straight for him. It was as if she had been waiting for him.

Spencer blushed and recoiled. He was staring at this beautiful woman, and he was sure it would unnerve her, but he never looked away, nor did she.

The ship slowly pulled away from the dock gathering speed as it turned to the open water of the Atlantic Ocean. Spencer waved his hands frantically. He shouted for them to stop the ship, that it was doomed. He watched until she became a white speck on the deck of a small toy boat.

+++

Spencer sat up in bed. He glanced around at the drab room. Sunlight streamed through the cracks in the venetian blinds casting strange shadows on the floor. He rolled over on the side of the bed and ran his hands through his hair. At least it was different this time. In this dream, he didn't drown or have to watch her run desperately down hallways trying to escape from the water. He reached for his wristwatch lying on the bed stand. It was nearly 11:00 in the morning. "Damn!"

he muttered. The exhibit opened at nine o'clock, and here he was still in bed.

It was nearly noon when he walked through the front doors of the Olympia. It was a grand old building built just after the turn of the century. It's huge, cavernous rooms made it perfect for civic events and public exhibits like the Titanic display.

Spencer paid his money and entered the first room. The walls were covered with framed photographs and paintings. Display cases were arranged in winding rows to create a walkway that wound back and forth and then led eventually to the next room.

Spencer's pulse raced as he bent over the first showcase. It seemed as if he had waited for this moment all his life. As a child, he often wondered what it would be like to see artifacts from the Titanic. He played games with his friends and asked them if they could own one piece of history, what would it be? One said Hitler's shaving mug, another wanted Babe Ruth's bat. The answer to that question was easy for Spencer. He wanted just about anything from the Titanic, and in particular, a bottle of wine. He wasn't quite sure why, he just wanted to see it on his mantle.

He peered through the glass. Lying neatly in the left-hand corner was a five-dollar bill, series 1902. Beside it was a one-cent Indian-head dated 1891. Near the bottom of the display was a faded and torn document. Spencer leaned closer. It was a stock certificate for the Witching Waves Company, and to the left of that, was a one-dollar silver certificate dated 1899.

"Damn," he muttered aloud. He smiled, scanned the case again and moved to the next one. Inside was a four by five-inch baggage label from the White Star Line. It was light blue with yellow markings, slightly tattered, but clearly readable.

Beside it was a man's pipe with tobacco still inside the bowl, and a blue and gold porcelain dinner plate with interlocking letters in the middle that spell out the initials of the parent company: The Oceanic Steam Navigation Company.

Spencer walked slowly across the room. There were bowls and jars and parts of the ship. There was a decanter with the etched white star flag, a small porthole, binoculars, and a man's wool suit vest. He turned the corner into the next room and found a deck bench, a megaphone, and a deck bell.

It was as if his whole life had led him to this day, this moment in time. And why the dreams? Why did they visit him every night? Was it the Titanic he saw every night in his dreams? And who was that goddess he chased, and, for that matter, why was he chasing her? He'd seen her a million times, always a side view or her back as she ran down corridors of the sinking ship. But today was different. Today he saw the face that went with that hauntingly beautiful body. And why did he have to travel to Memphis to finally see her?

Spencer slowly scanned the room, his eyes stopping on a small showcase near the back of the room. "Oh, my God," he muttered aloud. "It's the Holy Grail!" He walked slowly across the room, his eyes fixed on the display. He stopped in front of it and leaned over. Inside the case was a lone bottle filled with a dark red wine, the cork still intact. Spencer walked slowly around it studying its contents. It was just as he had imagined. The bottle was in pristine condition, and it was filled nearly to the top with dark, red nectar that was nearly a century old. Spencer smiled and turned silently to the people near him. He studied their blank faces and wondered why they weren't enraptured with this incredible treasure that lay before him. Nearly a half-hour passed before Spencer reluctantly walked away.

He turned the corner and entered another room. This one was filled with photographs displayed on corkboards and protected by glass. Spencer walked slowly, his eyes darting from one to the other. Some were taken during the construction of the ship, others on the day of her maiden voyage.

Since many of the photos were taken showing the exterior of the ship and were simply different angles, Spencer picked up his pace. It wasn't that he was bored, it was a sense of curiosity for what was waiting in the next room.

Spencer was nearly at the end of the wall when he noticed a faded photograph of a woman leaning against the railing. She was alone near the bow of the ship. Spencer moved closer. She was stunningly beautiful and had a familiar look about her. He bent over and studied the photo until it came to him. It was the girl in his dreams. There was that smile, that inexplicable smile that seemed directed to him. He couldn't explain it. It was as if he had known this woman all his life, and yet he felt a need to meet her for the first time. In all those dreams over the past months, he had never really seen her face, but somehow knew she would be the most beautiful woman he had ever met.

Then, it hit him. He stood erect and stared into the distance. Clearly, he had fallen in love with a woman who was dead. At the time this picture had been taken, she was a young adult, and that was decades ago. It didn't seem fair. How could he let himself fall in love with a woman who no longer existed?

Spencer felt a sense of loss. It was as if he had known her all his life and watched as she died in front of him.

From the corner of his eye, Spencer could see someone leaning over his shoulder.

"Quite a looker, ain't she?"

Spencer spun around. It was an old man leaning on a cane. He was dressed in an ill-fitting suit, his skin was pale, and he was bent over at the waist.

Spencer blushed. "Who do you mean?"

"The woman in the photograph," he said sharply. "Hell, I remember when they took that picture. Grandest lady I had ever seen."

"You were on the Titanic?" asked Spencer.

"Bradley McKinley's the name," he said, thrusting his hand towards Spencer. "You can call me Bradley. Everyone else does."

Spencer took his hand. "You're one of the few survivors still alive, aren't you?"

Bradley pointed his thumb over his shoulder. "They tell me there's some old geezer still alive somewhere up in Michigan, but chances are I'm the last one."

Spencer smiled and shook his hand even harder. "It's a pleasure to meet you, Mr. McKinley, 'er Bradley."

"I'll be eighty-nine next month."

"Damn!"

"Yeah, that's what I say," said Bradley.

"With all due respect, sir, I've been studying the Titanic all my life, and I don't remember anyone by your name," said Spencer. "In fact, I thought all of the survivors were dead."

"You'll never see my name in the history books," said Bradley. "You see my mother wanted to come to America really bad, and she managed to smuggle the two of us on board."

"At least, you got here," said Spencer.

"I did, but my mother wasn't as lucky. Seems they found out she wasn't a paying passenger, as if that should make a difference. Bastards wouldn't let her on a lifeboat."

Spencer stared at the man. "I don't believe it. All my life, I've read everything ever written about the Titanic, and now here I am among all these artifacts and talking to someone who was standing on her deck. If you don't mind my asking, what was she like?"

"The grandest thing anybody ever seen," said Bradley. "A body couldn't see from one end to the other."

Spencer's voice softened. "If you don't mind my asking, where were you on the night of the fourteenth?"

"Right out there on deck! Hell, I saw the iceberg gliding by. Didn't know at the time it was tearing a hole in the side of her. Probably wouldn't have thought of that iceberg quite as exciting, if I had known that."

Spencer turned to the photograph. "What do you know about her?"

Bradley leaned over and studied the photo for a moment. "She gave me a piece of candy just before that picture was snapped. Yes sir, she was quite a lady."

"Who took the photo?"

"Some photographer guy. Had one of them big cameras that set on a tripod and you slide the film in and out. I don't think he was taking a picture of her, he was more concerned with the Titanic. Not real sure he even noticed her."

Spencer stared at the photo.

"Do you know something about her?" asked Bradley.

Spencer said nothing.

"I say there, sonny…"

Spencer pointed at the printing below the picture. "Says here her name was Elizabeth York. I take it from the way she's dressed, she was third class."

Bradley's face turned sober. "She might have been dressed as third class, but that's not the way I remember it."

"What does that mean?" asked Spencer.

"I always thought she was some kind of queen or something of the sorts," said Bradley. "She had way too much class for third class."

"What do you mean?" asked Spencer.

"I don't know. It's just the way she handled herself, the way she walked and the way she talked. You know how you sometimes get a feeling about women? Well, my feeling was she was more than just third class."

"You said you saw her the day this photo was taken. Had you ever seen her before?"

"Like I said, she leaned over and handed me a piece of candy right before that picture was taken," said Bradley. "I'll never forget her."

"Well, I can certainly understand why," muttered Spencer.

"You got it bad, don't you?"

"It shows?"

"You're not the first to fall in love with that pretty face. Knew a man once who insisted I give him her phone number. Wouldn't accept the fact that she is no longer alive."

"Do you know anyone who works here?" asked Spencer.

"Well, technically, I do," said Bradley. "They pay me chicken feed to hang around here and talk with the people. Why?"

"I'd give anything for a copy of that picture."

Bradley motioned for Spencer to follow him. "That's not a problem. We store all these photos on a computer. I can print you a copy in no time."

Spencer had a look of surprise. "You can?"

"Hey, just because I'm old doesn't mean I can't run a computer," said Bradley. He sat down at the keyboard, brought up a file and soon printed a copy of the photo.

Scott Fields

Spencer watched as the copy emerged from the printer. He picked up the finished copy and smiled.

"Elizabeth York," muttered Spencer.

Bradley slowly shook his head. "I'll tell you the same thing I told that other guy, she went down with the ship. She's been dead for a long time."

Spencer heard nothing. "I've seen this woman before," he muttered aloud.

"That's impossible," said Bradley. "Even if she had survived, more than likely she would have died by now."

"No, I didn't see her in person. I mean I've seen her in a picture somewhere before today."

"Don't doubt that a bit," said Spencer. "That photo you got there in your hands came out of some magazine. We just fixed it up a bit for the display."

Spencer lightly folded the picture in half and started for the door. "Thanks for the information, Bradley."

"Any time, sonny," he said. "In fact, if you ever need to know anything else, I'm always around here telling lies."

+++

It was late afternoon when Spencer emerged from a display on the second floor. He strolled over to the edge of the balcony and leaned on the railing. He stared blankly across the lower level. Who was this Elizabeth York and what was she doing on the Titanic? She obviously was not married; her name would have appeared as Mrs. York. Why was she coming to America? Was she running to someone or away from something or somebody?

It seemed so pointless to ponder the questions, to consider her existence. She lived and died a tragic death decades ago. Why let the imagination drift back over the ages to a time long before he had even been born and consider what she must have been like?

Spencer turned around and leaned against the railing.

"Good day, Miss York," he softly muttered.

"Good day to you, Mr. Ellington."

"I was wondering if you would be free for dinner tonight?"

"Mr. Ellington, are you asking me for a date?"

"It's just that I'm all alone on this glamorous and romantic sea-going vessel and would greatly appreciate the company of such a beautiful lady."

A woman bumped into Spencer causing him to nearly lose his balance. He turned and studied the display cases scattered across the floor just below him.

Near the far end of the building, a woman hurried through the crowd. Out of the corner of his eye, Spencer picked up a familiar sight. He stood erect as he watched the woman weave in and out of the mass of people. Suddenly, he could feel his heart pounding in his chest. It couldn't be. Elizabeth York died on a cold night in April in 1912. This woman who moved so gracefully and effortlessly before his eyes was simply a modern-day look-a-like. She was someone who simply came to spend an afternoon visiting and enjoying a historical exhibit.

Spencer hurried to the other end of the balcony. What if it was her? Stranger things have happened. Nobody really knows what happens after death. Besides, what about the dreams he's been having? The dreams that never go away, the dreams that happen every night.

The woman stopped near the doorway. She was frozen in her tracks as if she had forgotten something and was trying to remember. Spencer leaned over the railing, as far as he dared.

Then, it happened. The woman turned and stared back at Spencer, as if she had known all along he was there on the balcony watching her. What did she want? Why was she smiling at him? It was as if she was waiting for him to come to her.

Spencer bolted across the balcony and down the stairs. He had to talk to her, to find out who she was. There was a connection, he was sure of that. She was somehow connected to the picture and to his dreams.

He hit the main floor and started across the room, weaving through the crowd of people that seemed to all be heading in his direction. He stopped near the doorway and searched the area. She was nowhere to be found. Maybe she was waiting for him outside. He bolted out the door and into the street, scanning in every direction. She had disappeared.

# Chapter Two

It was just after nine in the morning when Charlie Stenger was called into his bosses' office. Charlie had worked as an adjuster for the Mutual Insurance Company for nearly twenty years, and he was confident that today he would get the promotion he so well deserved.

By the age of twelve, Charlie had stopped growing leaving him just a little over five feet tall. At forty years of age, Charlie blamed everything on his lack of height, including his lack of promotions and his lack of dates. But today was different. Today, he will move up on the corporate ladder and with that accomplishment he was sure that women would soon follow.

"Charlie, my boy, have a seat," said Mr. Gibbs, pointing to an empty chair just in front of his desk.

Charlie smiled and took a seat. "Thank you, sir."

"I suppose you're wondering why I called you in here."

Charlie smiled again. "Well, I have a pretty good idea."

"What's that?"

"Well, Mike Stoughten retired last month, and I was hoping I might…"

"Money is tight right now, Charlie. Even you see it at your end of the business. And whenever that happens, budget cuts are just around the corner. Do you see where I'm going with this, Charlie?"

"Not really. I thought I was…"

"We're moving you down into records, Charlie. Now, I know you've been with us for nearly twenty years and this is just like starting over, but I've got to tell you, it's better than losing your job."

"Well, I suppose…"

"Report to Hastings down there, and he will get you started," said Mr. Gibbs, getting to his feet and thrusting out his hand. "Welcome to the team."

Charlie took his hand and wondered why he was being welcomed to the team he had been a part of for so many years. It sounded like a canned speech he gave to everyone.

Jim Hastings had spent his entire career in the records department. Being an entry-level position in the company, nobody was quite sure why he had never been promoted. Some said it was because he liked his job and had, in fact, refused various promotions over the years, others said it was because of his enormous weight. Jim was less than six feet tall and weighed over three hundred pounds. He had admitted on more than one occasion that he preferred the seclusion that Records provided.

Charlie found his way down a darkened stairway to the basement floor. He stopped in front of a wooden door that had the letters, "RECO" on it with faded outlines of three missing letters. He opened the door, and in the dim light could see a big man sitting at an old wooden desk that butted up against another desk. He was staring at the monitor of a computer. Surrounding them were rows and rows of metal file cabinets with huge books that resembled scrapbooks stacked in piles on the floor.

"Hastings?" blurted Charlie.

"You must be Stenger," said Jim, without turning around, "been expecting you."

"You knew I was going to be demoted?"

"Known it for over a week," said Jim. "Bet Gibbs didn't tell you that you took a twenty percent hit in your pay, did he?"

"Huh?"

"Just as I thought. He's got no balls for giving bad news," said Jim. "Have a seat. It should be still warm. The last guy sat there for a half of a day fuming about the pay cut and finally quit. You're not gonna quit on me, are you?"

Charlie walked over to the desk and sat down in a metal swivel chair. It squawked as he fell backwards in the chair. "I can't quit now, I have twenty years in the company."

"The last guy had thirty-five," said Jim. "What did you do to get committed to purgatory?"

Charlie searched the room. "Can't imagine."

"I heard the last guy got caught screwing Amy McPherson, the boss's secretary. That would have been worth the price of admission. Ever see her?"

"Can't say as I have," said Charlie. "Spent most of my time on the road. Only in the office on the weekends."

"She had a set of knockers you wouldn't believe and wore miniskirts with no underwear underneath. And that guy got to bang her. Some guys get all the luck. Hell, I would have eaten one of her turds just to see where it came from." Jim leaned back and turned to Charlie. "You married?"

"Not anymore."

"I, myself, never found the right girl," said Jim. "But then again, I'm getting along just fine by myself."

Charlie reached under the table and pushed the start button on his computer. "What do we do around here?"

Jim pointed across the room. "See all those file cabinets. They are full of old records that date before 1973 when Mutual bought their first computer. Our job is to input all those old files."

Charlie studied the main menu that appeared on his screen. "What should I do now?"

"Just play around on the computer for now," said Jim. "We'll get together later in the day."

Charlie did just that. He played on the computer until he was bored. It was late in the afternoon when Charlie found a particular file in the computer.

Charlie's eyes were fixed on the screen. "Hey, Jim. Here's some interesting stuff. The top ten largest pay outs by the company."

"How did you find that? You're in privileged files that require access codes."

"I was weaned on computers," said Charlie, then paused. "Whoa, Nelly! Here's one that goes back to 1915. Some Duke from England filed a claim for fifty million dollars. Can you imagine what that translates into in today's money?"

"I remember reading about that one," said Jim. "I think he had some jewelry stolen from him. Imagine the investigation on that one?"

"Too bad I wasn't around back then," said Charlie. "If it had been my case, we wouldn't have paid out a dime. I'd seen to that, all right."

"How can you be so sure?"

"There's a way around any claim to get out of it," said Charlie. "You just have to dig deep enough until you find the right dirt."

Jim struggled to his feet. "I'll take your word for it, but right now it's time to go home. You coming?"

Charlie kept his eyes on his computer. "I'm going to stick around for a while. See you in the morning."

It was nearly seven in the evening when Charlie sat down in his recliner with a sandwich and a beer. He pointed the remote at his television and the seven o'clock news began. It was near the end of the broadcast when a particular story caught Charlie's attention.

"Headed for the auction block is this rare diamond ring reported to be worth in the neighborhood of over ten million dollars," said the newscaster. "Its origin is unknown, but rumors have it that it once belonged to royalty nearly a century ago."

Charlie leaned forward as they flashed a photo of the ring onto the screen. "Damn, that looks familiar," he said aloud.

"What makes this story even more bizarre is that this ring supposedly went to the bottom of the ocean back in 1912 with the ill-fated Titanic," said the newscaster. He turned to his co-anchor. "Makes you wonder how it got back into circulation, doesn't it?"

Charlie got to his feet and shook his fist at the TV. "I'm going to do more than wonder, wise guy. Unless I miss my guess, this has become my business."

The next morning, for the first time in his life, Charlie sped to work. He nearly ran down the steps and pushed open the door.

"Morning, Jim," he said, sitting down at his desk.

"My, aren't we full of piss and vinegar this morning," said Jim.

"That fifty million dollar claim back in 1915, where would I find the poop on that?"

Jim pointed at a lone wooden file cabinet. "Third drawer down. It's the file called Duke of Devonshire."

Charlie thumbed through the files. "Was he really a duke?"

"As I recall, he claimed his wife's jewelry went down on the Titanic. Sounds a little convenient to me."

"Yeah, especially since a piece of the collection showed up at an auction," said Charlie.

"What?'

"Well, I'm not sure of anything. I just saw something on the news last night about it. That's all."

"I always thought that sounded a little fishy," said Jim. "Bet they did too, seeing as how they didn't pay off until 1915 three years after it happened."

Charlie opened the file and thumbed through the yellowed pages until he came across a faded photograph of an array of jewelry spread out over crushed velvet.

"That's it! That's the same jewelry as the ring I saw on TV last night."

Jim got up from his chair and leaned over his desk to see. "Are you sure?"

"I'm positive. Says here his maid was tied up by the thieves who stole the jewelry and overheard one of them say that they needed to hurry up because the Titanic was due to leave."

"Do you suppose they believed that story?" asked Jim.

"Are you going to call a duke a liar? Couldn't he have you beheaded or some such shit?"

"Good point."

Charlie leaned back and smiled. "If all that jewelry went down on the Titanic, how did this ring show up? Makes you wonder if it never went down to the bottom of the ocean, where is it and who has had it all these years?"

Jim sat back down. "You sound more like an investigator than a records guy."

"This one I'm doing on my own time," said Charlie. "This could be my meal ticket out of here."

 # CHAPTER THREE

Spencer rolled over in bed. He got in late the night before from the long drive from Memphis. He glanced at the clock near his bed, it was after ten. Funny, it didn't seem that late, and yet the room was already starting to heat up from the late morning sun.

It was another night of weird dreams. At least this time, he had a name to go with the face. Elizabeth York, or at least a woman, who looked like Elizabeth York, was running down corridors as always, but this time another man was pursuing her. In the dream, he catches her and tries to strangle her.

Spencer rolled over and sat on the edge of the bed. He reached to the nightstand for the picture of Elizabeth. He couldn't believe how much his heart ached for a woman who had died years before his own father was born. It didn't seem normal to be thinking about her, but he couldn't help himself. She was beautiful, much more beautiful than he had ever known.

Somehow, Spencer knew there was more to this than he understood. It was more than just a picture of a woman who lived a long time ago. If that was all there was to it, he wouldn't be having these dreams that included her every night.

Spencer studied the picture. She was standing at the railing looking away from the ship just as she was in his dream. It was much too incredibly coincidental, and yet there was something else about this photo. It was as if he had seen it before. That couldn't be possible, and yet he owned nearly every book written about the Titanic. Perhaps he once saw it in one of his books.

Spencer dug through a pile of books until he found one that was a gallery of photos taken of the Titanic. He laid the book on his desk and turned on the light. He studied the photos as he slowly thumbed through the book. In the beginning were pictures taken during the construction of the vessel from the laying of the keel to the hanging of the chandeliers. Then came the pictures taken as the passengers boarded her for her first and only voyage.

It was near the end of the book that he found it. It was the photo of Elizabeth standing near the railing. He grabbed the copy he had brought from the exhibit and held them side-by-side. They were identical.

That explained it. He must have seen this photo years ago and simply forgot about it. That's why it seemed so familiar when he saw it at the exhibit. Spencer smiled. Maybe he wasn't going crazy after all.

Just then, there came a soft knock on the door. Spencer slipped on a pair of sweatpants and opened the door.

"Morning, Spencer," said Casey. "Hope I'm not disturbing you."

"Not at all," he said. "Come on in."

Casey stepped inside and glanced around the room. "Knew you got in late last night, so I waited before knocking on your door. How was your trip?"

"Wonderful," he said with a smile. "Absolutely wonderful."

She slowly walked across the room to his desk and stared at the pictures. "Who's this?"

"This is the most beautiful woman in the world," he said with a smile.

Casey leaned forward. "She is beautiful. I'll give you that. Who is she?"

"I'm not real sure. All I know is she was on the Titanic," said Spencer. He pointed at one of the pictures. "This is a copy of a photo in the Titanic Exhibit. This other one is the same picture in one of my books."

Casey studied the two pictures. "They're not the same," she said.

"What do you mean?"

"They're two different photographs," she said. "In the copy you brought from the exhibit, she has her right hand on her chest. In this one, neither hand is visible."

Spencer sat down at the desk. "I guess you're right," he muttered. "Seems strange though. Everything else is identical. Maybe two different people snapped pictures within seconds of each other."

Casey pointed at a young boy running on the deck behind her. "That boy looks as if he's running at full speed, and yet there's no difference between the two photos. Even if you allowed two seconds for her to put her hand down, you would notice a difference when you look at the boy."

"I suppose you're right," said Spencer. "Then how do you explain these two photos? They're obviously the same photo, and yet her hands only show in the one."

"Why are we having this conversation anyway? I've never seen you so riled up," she said.

Spencer leaned back in his chair. "I can't explain it, but I feel as if I've known this woman, and stranger still I get this feeling she's trying to contact me."

Casey frowned. "Without doubt, the woman is dead."

"That's the next problem on the list. I saw her at the exhibit."

"You saw the woman in this photo?"

"I know how this must sound, but I'm telling you it was her. I was standing on the balcony when I saw her leaving the exhibit."

"Did you see her face straight on?" asked Casey.

"Not exactly."

"How far away were you from her?"

Spencer blushed. "Well, she was across the room about fifty yards."

"And yet you're positive it was a woman who should by now be over a hundred years old?"

"Kinda crazy, ain't it?"

Casey paused. "Somehow I get the idea you have feelings for this woman."

Spencer turned to the photos. "Yeah…I guess I do."

"What's her name?"

"Elizabeth York."

"Strange."

"What's strange?"

"Such a classy woman dressed in rags, and that look on her face…it just doesn't figure. That's not the face of a woman who has spent her life worrying about money."

"Kind of a mystery, isn't it?"

"Well, I can see one way you can tell if those are the same photos," said Casey. "Look behind her. There is a clock on the deck, and it looks like it says ten 'til nine. Now, if you can just see the second hand."

Spencer leaned forward. "I can't make them out."

"I know who can," said Casey. "Take them down to the police station and give them to your brother. He can have them blown up so they can be read."

"Think he would do it?"

"If he's not too busy."

Spencer jumped to his feet. "Can you call him while I get ready?"

"You're worse than a kid."

"I'll tell you what," said Spencer. "For the first time in years, I feel like a kid."

"I hate to do this to you, but your ex is coming over here to see you in about an hour," said Casey.

The smile disappeared from his face. "What does she want?"

"I don't know. She didn't say."

"She got everything I own and half my pay, what more could she want?"

"A pint of blood, maybe?"

Spencer grabbed a towel and threw it around his neck. "I'm taking a shower, and then I'm out of here. Tell her I'll be back later on."

 # CHAPTER FOUR

Tyler Ellington had proudly served as a police officer for nearly fifteen years. If he kept his nose clean and stayed out of trouble, he could retire with full benefits in five years. He dreamed of getting a part time job as a security officer or a night watchman and spend his free time bowling in the winter and playing golf in the summer. But it was just a dream and depended on the next five years. He was on duty that day filling out paperwork when Spencer walked in.

"Did Casey call you?" asked Spencer.

Tyler got up from his desk. "Have you lost your mind?"

"Maybe just a little bit."

"You're in love with a woman who died on the Titanic, and you say just a little bit?"

Spencer blushed. "Well...

"And then to top it off, you think she's alive today and you say she looks just like she did ninety years ago!"

"I guess when you put it that way..."

Tyler held out his hand. "Let me see those photos."

Spencer slipped the two photos from a manila envelope and handed them to his brother.

"Wow! She's quite a looker," said Tyler. "I can see why you have the hots for her, but Spencer, my dear brother, she can't possibly look this good today."

Spencer pointed at the picture. "I'm telling you I saw that woman, and she looks just like that."

Tyler paused deliberating whether to debate the issue or not.

"Now what was it you wanted blown up?" asked Tyler.

Spencer pointed at a small white spot on both of them. "That's a clock on deck. I need to see the second hand."

"You're wasting your time," said Tyler.

"Why?"

"They're two different pictures, anybody can see that."

"See the boy behind her?" asked Spencer. "He's running across the deck, and he's frozen in the same position in both pictures."

Tyler leaned closer. "I'll be damned," he muttered. "I'll tell you what. We have the best man in the business. Let me give these to him, and we'll soon see."

Tyler disappeared behind a door for a moment and soon returned. "Casey tells me she was about a mile away when you saw her."

"She wasn't that far away."

"She also tells me you've got it bad for this girl."

Spencer smiled. "Yeah, I guess you could say that," he said. "I can't really explain it. It's more than just an infatuation. It's like she's trying to contact me."

Tyler smirked. "Who's trying to contact you?"

"The woman in these photos," said Spencer.

"The woman who lived ninety years ago or the one you saw the other day?"

"That's the problem," said Spencer. "I think they're one and the same. I think Elizabeth York is trying to...tell me something, and that was her the other day."

"So, she's come back to life, is that it?"

"I don't know whether you would call it that. I think it's more like an apparition."

Tyler laid his hand on Spencer's shoulder. "Hey, brother, I'm just a dumb cop. I don't have any idea what an apparition is."

"Ghost," said Spencer. "I think what I saw was a ghost."

Tyler paused. "Man, you've been sniffing too much model cement."

A door opened, and a man dressed in a white lab coat stepped inside. He handed Tyler a manila envelope. "You owe me, Tyler," he said, turned and walked away.

Tyler took the envelope and walked across the room to a desk piled high with paperwork. He pulled out the contents and laid them on the desk. He laid the original two photos on the desk side-by-side. He then placed the two blowups under each one. The clock was clearly visible in each blowup, and the second hand was pointing at the eight.

"Well, I'll be," said Tyler. "These two photos are the same."

"Then how do you explain the fact that her hand is near her chest in this one and not in the other?"

"Maybe you're right," said Tyler. "Maybe she is trying to reach you. Maybe the answer is right here in front of us."

Spencer leaned over the pictures. "It must have something to do with her hand. Everything else is the same."

Tyler paused. "That's it! She's pointing at something. It looks as if she's pointing at the pendant around her neck."

"Wonder what's so precious about that?" asked Spencer.

"Maybe it's worth a lot of money."

"I hardly think someone riding in third class would be wearing valuable jewelry," said Spencer. "It must be something else."

"Maybe she's pointing at the clock that's behind her. Maybe the time of day is important."

"Ten 'til nine? What could be significant about that time? Obviously, it's in the morning, there would be no light otherwise."

Tyler picked up the picture and held it to the light. "There are markings on that pendant," he said. "I wonder what they are."

Spencer moved closer. "I can't make it out."

Tyler opened his desk drawer, pulled out a magnifying glass and handed it to Spencer.

Spencer positioned it over the photo. "It's some kind of design," he said.

"That's not a design," said Tyler. "That's a family crest. Here, give it to me and we'll see if we can find anything on the computer."

Tyler launched his Internet browser, and found a site listing coats of arms and family crests. He scanned the list searching for a match to the one on the pendant.

"Bingo," said Tyler.

"Did you find it?" asked Spencer.

"I think you have a problem," said Tyler. "That pendant belonged to some duchess in England. You're in love with a crook."

Spencer leaned over his shoulder. "That can't be."

"Then why did she have the pendant? It belonged to the duchess."

"I don't know, maybe she was friends with the duchess."

"People from third class didn't have friends in first class," said Tyler. "Naw, what you have here is simple larceny. Better get yourself a new girlfriend."

"I don't believe it," said Spencer. "There's got to be a reason for her wearing that pendant."

"Yeah, she stole it."

Spencer dropped into a chair. "Just my luck, I fall in love with a woman who is a thief and lived and died years before even dad was born."

The smile on Tyler's face disappeared. "Sorry, man."

Spencer stared out the window. "You know, when I got married, I knew within the first month it wasn't going to work out. We weren't even close to being compatible. Funny how people change after marriage. But I stuck it out, God knows why. I stuck it out, until I just couldn't take another fight, another disappointment, another day with that woman."

"I know it's none of my business, but how could you fall in love with a photo of a woman who lived all those years ago?" Tyler asked. "You have to admit, it's kinda weird."

"I don't know," said Spencer. "I tried to let it go. God knows I tried. I told myself over and over that it makes no sense. There's no future in this. I had nearly convinced myself too when it happened. I know how it must sound, but I'm as sure as anything I know, that was her I saw in the crowd."

Tyler leaned back in his chair. "So where do you go from here? My gut tells me she's a thief. I don't know who you saw the other day, but your Elizabeth York is dead. Either she went down on the Titanic or died of old age. Either way, she's dead."

Spencer got to his feet. "I know it's hard to believe, but that was her I saw the other day," he said with a smile.

"Besides, if you want something hard to believe, explain these two photos."

Tyler smiled and shrugged his shoulders, as Spencer walked away.

+++

Gina Ellington poured herself a cup of coffee and took a seat at the kitchen table across from Casey. She was an attractive woman with blonde hair that cascaded over her shoulders. She was thin, yet generously endowed with feminine charm.

"How is he?" asked Gina.

"Spencer? He's fine," said Casey.

"I suppose you're wondering what I'm doing over here."

"That has crossed my mind."

Gina sipped her coffee. "I just wanted to talk to him," she said and paused. "I want to see if he's doing all right."

Casey smiled. "Come on, girl. You can talk to me. What's going on?"

Gina leaned back in her chair. "I don't know, Casey. I just can't believe we're all through. We had such a good thing going."

"You still love the guy, don't you?"

"It shows?"

"It's written all over your face."

"Why is it I can love a man so much and can't stand to live with him?" said Gina. "Can you tell me that?"

Casey poured herself another cup of coffee. "To tell you the truth, I don't think they're trainable. Sometimes, I could kill the one I got."

"I never thought I would say this, but I miss him," said Gina. "He leaves his clothes on the floor, he slops up the bathroom, he's never remembered my birthday, not once, and yet I miss him."

Casey laughed. "If it makes you feel any better, they're all alike, every last one of them. Barely toilet-trained slobs who think of no one but themselves."

"Why do they have to be that way?"

"I don't know," said Casey. "And the worst part is you can't change them. Oh, they're nice once in a while, especially when they need something from you, but it only lasts for a short time. If you don't mind my asking, who divorced who?"

"I don't know. I guess it was a mutual thing. We had another one of our fights, but this one was the granddaddy of all. One thing led to another and before you knew it, he was talking divorce and I was agreeing with him."

"But you went through with it," said Casey.

"I still don't believe it," said Gina. "It was just another fight. It's just that this one went a little too far."

Gina stopped talking as the back door opened and Spencer stepped inside. It was the first time they had confronted one another since the divorce was final. Spencer first looked at Casey and then Gina. The air was thick.

"Hi," he said, still looking at Gina.

Gina forced a smile. "Hi."

Casey took a deep breath and got to her feet. "Well, I guess it's time for me to get lost."

"Oh, no," said Spencer. "Stick around."

Casey started for the door. "No, thank you. I've got dirt to scratch and eggs to lay. Let me know how it turns out," she said and closed the door behind her.

Spencer took a seat across from Gina. "How have you been?"

"Fine, and you?"

Spencer stiffened. "Back has been acting up, but other than that I can't complain."

"Ice it down," she said. "Don't use heat like you did that one time. Just made it worse."

"How's your mother doing?" he asked.

"She's fine. Might have to go in for an operation though."

"Oh, yeah? What for?

Gina smiled. "You don't want to know."

"Oh," mumbled Spencer. "So, what brings you over here? I'm sure you're not interested in swapping recipes."

"I don't know, I just wanted to know how you were doing," she said, glancing out the window.

"C'mon, Gina, I know you better than that. There's something on your mind. Now what is it?"

"I was just wondering…"

"What?"

"I was wondering if you would like to move back home."

Spencer's mouth dropped. "Are you serious?"

"Other people do it," she said. "I was reading a story just this morning about all the couples who can't be married, but make great friends."

Spencer leaned back in his chair, his face flushed. "That sounds great, but…"

"You've got a girlfriend, don't you?"

"Well, kinda."

"I should have known," she barked. "The ink isn't even dry on our divorce paper and you're already banging somebody else."

"You don't understand," said Spencer. "She's not…"

Gina jumped to her feet and started for the door. "I don't want to hear any more. Your dick is doing the talking."

"She went down on the Titanic," blurted Spencer.

Gina opened the door and turned to him. "I don't care who she went down on. I'm outta here."

Spencer was staring at the closed door when Casey walked in.

"I screwed the bitch on that one," he said.

"So I heard. She didn't give you much of a chance to explain."

"For a moment there, I thought I was married again."

Casey smiled. "I have good news."

"I could use it," said Spencer.

"I have your job interview rescheduled for tomorrow afternoon," she said. "It wasn't easy, but I got it done."

"Thanks, Casey," said Spencer, getting to his feet. "You're a doll. Right now, I have some stuff to do. I'll be back later."

+++

It was nearly 7:00 in the evening when Tyler got home from work. Spencer was sitting in a recliner and Casey was on the couch when he entered the living room. He stopped in the middle of the room, looked at both Casey and Spencer and then dropped onto the couch.

"Now let me get this straight," said Tyler. "I'm feeding you and putting a roof over your head, and I come home and find you alone with my wife sitting in my favorite chair."

"Don't forget I'm watching the news on your television," said Spencer.

"Jesus, I'm a cop. I should arrest you."

"By the way, what did you guys find out from those photos?" asked Casey.

"You didn't tell her?" asked Tyler.

"She's wearing jewelry that doesn't belong to her," said Tyler.

"What are you saying?" asked Casey.

"I'm saying I think she's a…"

Just then Spencer waved his hand over his head and leaned forward in his chair. He pointed at the TV. "Holy Christ! Look at that ring!"

Tyler and Casey turned to the television. There lying on white silk was a diamond ring considered to be one of the most valuable rings in the world. It was on its way to an auction house in New York.

"Does that ring look familiar?" asked Spencer. He grabbed the photo lying on the table next to him and handed it to Tyler. He studied first the image on the screen and then the photo.

"That's it!" said Tyler. "That's the ring on your girlfriend's finger!"

"That's what I thought, but it just didn't seem possible," said Spencer.

"Yeah, since it went down with the ship, what's it doing at an auction, and where has it been all these years?"

Spencer held up the photos side-by-side. He glanced at the one and then studied the other with her exposed hand.

He jumped to his feet. "That's it! That's the message she's been trying to send me. It's the ring. We thought she was pointing to the pendant, but all the time she was trying to show us the ring."

Tyler glanced at the photos. "Okay, let's assume that you're right, but what does she want you to do? You obviously can't afford to buy it?"

"I think she's trying to warn me about something."

"Warn you about what?" asked Tyler.

"I don't know," said Spencer. "I guess that's for me to find out."

Casey edged forward on her chair. "I hate to burst your bubble on this guys, but I think you're missing one very important point. She's a thief. Not only did she steal that pendant, but she, obviously, stole that ring as well. She might be beautiful, but she doesn't look like she could afford a ring like that."

"So, what's your point?" asked Spencer.

"How can you trust a thief, especially one who's been dead that many years?"

Tyler smiled. "She's got you there."

"I have to go back to Memphis," said Spencer turning to Tyler. "Can you go with me?"

"I don't know. Why?"

"There's an old man down there who knows more than he's telling."

Tyler smiled at Casey. "Wanna come along?"

"I don't think so," she said. "I have too much to do right here at home, but you two go right ahead."

"Tomorrow morning?" asked Spencer.

Tyler shrugged his shoulders. "Tomorrow morning it is."

 # CHAPTER FIVE

The Titanic Exhibit had drawn crowds of people since it opened to the public, and today was no different. Tyler and Spencer weaved their way through the crowds until they reached the exhibit where Spencer had last seen Bradley McKinley. A young woman wearing a badge stood next to the display case.

"There was an old man here who claimed to be a survivor of the Titanic," said Spencer.

"That would be Bradley," she said with a smile.

"Yeah, that's his name," said Spencer. "Where is he?"

"Called in sick," she said. "Of course, at his age he has every right. Eighty-nine years old, you know."

"I need to talk to him. Can you tell me where he lives?"

"Oh, you'd have to ask the manager," she said. She turned and pointed. "That's him over there."

"Thanks," said Spencer and made his way across the room to a large overweight man standing near another display.

"I understand you're the manager," said Spencer. "I wonder if you could help me."

The man dropped the clipboard he was holding to his side. "I'll certainly try."

"I'm looking for Bradley McKinley, and they tell me he called in today."

"I took the call. Said he didn't feel well. Why? Is there a problem?"

"I need to talk to him," said Spencer. "I wonder if you might give me his home address."

He slowly shook his head. "Oh, I can't do that. It's against policy."

Tyler stepped forward and reached into his pocket. He withdrew his badge and showed it to the man. "We just need to ask him a few questions," said Tyler.

He stepped back. "Is he in some kind of trouble?"

"No, sir," said Tyler. "Just routine questions."

The manager scribbled down an address and handed it to Spencer. "Hope everything is all right. We're kinda proud of old Bradley around here, seeing as how he's the only survivor of the..."

"Thanks a lot," said Tyler, turning and walking away.

"Kinda short with him, weren't you?" asked Spencer.

"A guy like that gets cranked up and we'll never shut him up. Besides, I want to go see this Bradley guy."

Bradley lived in an older neighborhood on the eastside of town. The houses were Victorian, massive in size and belonging to another era. Spencer stopped in front of Bradley's house. It was as they expected, neat and clean with a well-cared for lawn and shrubs. They got out of the car and walked to the front door. Spencer knocked several times before it opened.

Bradley paused as he stared at the two men. "May I help you?" he finally asked.

Spencer pointed at himself. "Bradley, do you remember me?"

Bradley scowled for a moment and then his face lit up. "You're that young man who was at the exhibit," he said and swung open the door. "Come on in."

Tyler and Spencer stepped inside.

"Have a seat," said Bradley.

"My name is Spencer, and this is my brother, Tyler."

"Nice to meet you," said Bradley taking Tyler's hand.

Spencer sat on the edge of his chair. "They said you called in sick today. I hope it's nothing serious."

Bradley rubbed his forehead. "I think it's more old age than anything. Just wasn't feeling so good today. I've slowed down a lot since turning eighty a while back."

Spencer glanced at Tyler.

"I'm sorry to bother you," said Spencer, but we've come a long way to ask you a few questions."

"Fire away."

"When we were last together, I was asking you questions about Elizabeth York."

"I remember."

"I got the feeling there were things you weren't telling me."

Bradley smiled. "Tell me, sonny, why are you interested in Elizabeth York?"

"I'm in love with her. That's why."

"She's been dead for years."

Spencer leaned back in his chair. He thrummed his fingers on the arm of the chair trying to decide whether or not to continue.

"Elizabeth York is trying to communicate with me," said Spencer.

"What did you say?" asked the old man.

"Elizabeth York is sending me messages," said Spencer. "I don't know why or even what the messages mean, but I have a strong feeling she's trying to tell me something."

"What kind of messages is she sending to you?"

Spencer pulled out the two photographs. "See this photo? This is the one you made for me when I was here. This other photo is from a book I have."

Bradley stared at the two pictures. "They're identical. So what?"

"Look again," said Spencer.

The old man took a closer look. "Oh, her hand is in this picture and not in this one," he said. "They are two different photos."

"That's what I thought until I did a little digging. The first thing I noticed is the little boy running in the background. Notice how he's frozen in the same spot."

Bradley glanced at one photo and then at the other. "Isn't that strange? It would appear he's frozen. He's obviously running, yet he did not move from one photo to the other."

Spencer pointed at the photo. "Notice the clock in the background? We had that area of the photos blown up."

Bradley smiled. "Let me guess. The second hand is the same on both clocks."

"If these two pictures are not the same, then they were taken simultaneously," said Spencer.

"And yet they are different," muttered Bradley. "How do you suppose this is so?"

"There is no logical explanation for it," said Spencer. "I think she's trying to tell me something or to be more precise, I think she is trying to warn me about something. What it is, I have no idea."

Bradley was still looking at the two pictures. "I guess I forgot just how beautiful she was."

"You told me she gave you a piece of candy just before that picture was taken," said Spencer. "Somehow, I get the feeling you knew her better than that."

Bradley picked up one of the photos and leaned back in his chair. He stared into the hauntingly beautiful eyes of the face in the picture, his lips slowly moved as if he were having an intimate conversation.

"She was the most beautiful woman I've ever known," he said, his voice mellow almost raspy. "She walked with the grace of angels; her touch was as light as a summer wind. God help me, I loved that woman myself, and I was but a child. When she held me in her arms, it was as if God had taken me into His bosom. I can still feel her heartbeat."

Silence fell on the room. It was obvious to Spencer and Tyler that Bradley was lost in a river of memories.

"Elizabeth York didn't die on the Titanic, did she?" asked Spencer.

Bradley's face sobered. "Elizabeth York, or Elizabeth Longberry as I knew her, is gone now. With any luck, I'll soon meet my maker, and hopefully will be reunited with that wonderful woman."

"Why did she change her name?"

"Longberry is her married name. Although she did change her name…Smith or Jones or something like that."

Spencer shifted his weight and cleared his throat. "I don't mean to dispute your word, but according to records, Elizabeth York did go down on the Titanic."

"No, she didn't go down on the Titanic, but she wasn't a survivor either."

"I don't understand," said Spencer.

"You see, the only way to determine who died on the Titanic was to see who survived. If someone didn't report in, it was assumed they either drowned or froze to death in the icy waters. Elizabeth York didn't report in."

"Why?"

"Elizabeth was running to America to escape from an abusive husband. She told me stories of how he beat her and often kept her locked up so no other man could see her. When she survived the disaster, she recognized an opportunity for her to ensure her freedom, and that's how Elizabeth York died and Elizabeth Longberry came to be."

"That's incredible," muttered Spencer.

"An incredible story about an incredible woman," said Bradley.

"If you don't mind my asking, how did you come to know so much about Elizabeth York, or rather Elizabeth Longberry?" asked Spencer.

"My own mother wasn't quite as lucky. I remember it was a horribly cold night. We were on deck at the very moment the ship struck the iceberg, or rather grazed by it. I remember losing my balance as the ship heaved to port. We didn't think much of it, not much more than two people bumping into one another in a crowd. Chunks of ice showered onto the deck sliding in all directions. I remember picking up a piece and eating it as if it were candy. Imagine if you will, I ate a piece of the famous iceberg that sunk the Titanic. Quite a claim to fame."

"She didn't sink right away," said Spencer.

"I don't think anyone including the captain had any idea of the magnitude of the damage. We thought it was merely a close call. Little did we know she was mortally wounded and time was running out.

By the time the order was given to abandon ship, she was already listing to the starboard side and low in the water. Even as a small child, I recognized the gravity of the situation. We had the advantage of already being on deck unlike many of the other third-class passengers who could not escape from the lower decks. Mother and I were swept up in the crowds of women and children and found ourselves being ushered into one of the lifeboats."

"I've read several accounts that said the lifeboats were launched no ways near filled to capacity," said Spencer.

"You couldn't have slipped a mouse on that little boat if you tried," said Bradley. "I've read those stories myself. All I know is the one I was on was completely full. There were two sailors on board. They pushed us away from the Titanic and began to row, steering us away from the sinking ship. It became clearly obvious that we had too many souls on board. We were riding dangerously low in the water and taking on water at an alarming rate.

Then one of the sailors called out that someone would have to get off. Everyone went quiet for fear that it might be him or her, and then it happened. An old woman pointed at mother and declared that she was third class and should be the one to go just as if there are first and third-class tickets on a lifeboat. Even as a small child, I knew that my mother had just been given the death sentence. The sailor had no choice but to order her to disembark from the boat. He gave her one minute to make peace with her maker. I remember feeling outraged and yet grateful for the opportunity to say goodbye."

Bradley covered his eyes and wept.

"Mr. McKinley, you don't have to put yourself through this," said Tyler.

"You know in all these years, I've never told anybody about this. Oh, I have my stock stories I tell the Rotary Club and the wide-eyed faces that come to the exhibit, but not this stuff. These memories have been locked up for all these years."

Spencer leaned forward. "Mr. McKinley, I didn't mean for you to…"

"I remember my mother holding me close, and then looking me straight in the eyes. She told me that no matter what happened, she would always be with me. Even if she didn't make it, she would always be just a breath away. In all the years since that moment, I've never known the pain I felt on that night. She lightly kissed me on the forehead and climbed over the side of the boat. I hated those people who sentenced my mother to death."

"She hung there on the side of the boat for nearly thirty minutes. It was an act of desperation, but I tried to warm her hands by holding mine over hers. I'd like to think I gave her an extra minute or two. Finally, her shivering turned into convulsions and she slowly slipped away into the dark icy water. I remember watching the hands that I had tried so desperately to warm as they slipped beneath the surface of the ocean."

Tyler hung his head. "Dear God," he muttered.

Bradley grew silent as he collected his thoughts. He sat there for several minutes, and out of respect, neither Spencer nor Tyler said anything.

"No kid should ever experience that," said Bradley. "All those years ago, and it still bothers me. I can still see her face. It haunts me still today."

He paused for a moment.

"You ever heard of the expression that says something like when one door closes, God opens another?" asked Bradley.

"Well, there was another lady sitting in that boat watching all that went on. She immediately took me under her wing and eventually adopted me as her own. That lady was your Elizabeth York, my Elizabeth Longberry."

Spencer smiled. "That means I'm in love with your mother…an eighty-nine-year-old man's mother."

"Kinda sick, ain't it?" said Bradley.

"You need to pick on someone your own age," said Tyler.

"You're not the first to fall in love with that woman," said Bradley. "Most every man who ever met her, sooner or later would fall under her spell."

"So, you did indeed know Elizabeth York," said Spencer. "Why didn't you tell me sooner?"

"Oh, I don't know, some things are personal and should be kept that way, don't you agree?"

Spencer picked up one of the photographs and handed it to Bradley. "Your mother is wearing a ring in that photo. Can you tell me anything about it?"

Bradley held the picture under a lamp next to his chair. "That was quite possibly her most favorite possession. I always hoped I was her favorite, but I'm really sure that ring had the honor."

Tyler leaned forward. "Mr. McKinley, do you have any idea where she got the ring?"

Bradley paused and then smiled. "Now, I'm getting the idea that you two know more than you're telling."

"We have our reasons for asking," said Spencer.

"I have no idea where she got the ring. There were some things she kept private. In fact, I knew little of the time before I met her. She just didn't seem to want to talk about it."

"Whatever become of the ring?" asked Spencer.

"Shortly before she died, she gave it to me. Now, you can imagine how surprised I was, seeing as how this was her most favorite of all possessions. She told me to sell it after she was gone. Well, I just never had the heart to sell that ring, and then about five years ago someone broke into my house and stole it. Never saw it again. Why the interest in that ancient piece of jewelry?"

"That ancient piece of jewelry as you call it, is on the auction block and is considered to be one of the most valuable rings in history," said Tyler. "It's worth millions."

"Oh, my," said Bradley. "I knew it was pretty, but I didn't know it was that pretty. By the way, shouldn't we go to that auction? We could catch the guy who broke into my house."

"I'm afraid it isn't quite that easy," said Tyler. "That ring has been sold so many times in the last five years that the current owner has no idea it was stolen."

Bradley handed the photo back to Spencer, then leaned back in his chair. "So, tell me the truth. I was led to believe you were interested in Elizabeth York, and now it would appear you are more interested in the ring."

"No, no. It's nothing like that," said Spencer. "I believe she's trying to warn me about something that has to do with that ring. I just can't figure out what it is."

"Funny thing about that ring," said Bradley. "I always got the feeling there was more to it than that. There were things she said that made me suspect it was a part of a set. You know, like there was a necklace, bracelet and such. Don't know why. Never saw anything else but the ring. Just a feeling I had."

Spencer got to his feet, and Tyler followed.

"You've been a great help, Bradley," said Spencer, extending his hand. "But I think it's time we left you alone."

Tyler shook his hand as well. "I thoroughly enjoyed meeting you."

"You boys come back and see me and don't wait too long. Guys my age think twice about buying green bananas."

The boys opened the front door. Tyler stepped outside while Spencer stopped in the doorway. Bradley came over and grabbed Spencer by the arm. The smile on his face had disappeared. He had a wide-eyed look that sent a chill down Spencer's back.

"Look to your dreams," he said, his voice quivering. "Your senses are sometimes not to be trusted. The truth can sometimes be found in the whimsical senselessness of the mind at rest."

With that, he patted Spencer on the back of the hand and closed the door.

# CHAPTER SIX

Spencer turned the corner and started down the sidewalk. It was dark and the only light came from the streetlights at each corner. It was windy, and the back-and-forth motion of the tree branches cast eerie shadows. He was halfway down the block when he saw her. She was standing under the next streetlight with her back to him. She was dressed in a long white dress and long flowing brunette hair. She seemed impatient, as if she was waiting for someone.

Spencer came within twenty yards and stopped. She somehow looked familiar, but he couldn't be sure. Who was this woman and why was she here? He glanced around. It wasn't a very good part of town. It couldn't be all that safe for her to be there. Maybe he should wait with her just to be sure she remains safe, but then if she turned out to be a stranger, she was not going to want him around. Women don't trust a perfect stranger to be concerned for their safety.

He took a few steps closer and stopped again. There was something about her that made him want to move closer. He felt as if he knew her, and yet he was sure he had never met her before. Who was this woman? He had to find out.

From behind him, a car careened around the corner. The woman spun around in the direction of the screeching tires. No wonder he recognized her. It was Elizabeth York. She shielded her eyes and peered into the darkness. Spencer turned to see a dark sedan with its lights turned off speeding in her direction.

Spencer turned back to Elizabeth. By now, she was off the sidewalk and standing in the street. She was straining to see in the darkness, yet could not see that the sedan was heading towards her.

"Get out of the way!" he screamed and started to run in her direction. At the sound of his voice, she turned to him and smiled.

"You're in danger!" he shouted as he ran towards her. Her smile widened, her arms were now outstretched as she slowly ran towards Spencer. He ran faster screaming at her to go back, but to no avail. How could she still be smiling with a car travelling directly at her?

Spencer was within ten feet when the front of the car found its target. There was a loud thud and the sound of glass breaking. The impact sent Elizabeth flying through the air landing on the sidewalk over twenty feet away. Spencer slowed to a walk. He stepped onto the curb and slowly approached the lifeless body. Blood was smeared on the concrete where she slid after landing on the walk. He cautiously came closer until he was leaning over the body, when suddenly she sat straight up with blood pouring from her mouth. She pointed in his direction and laughed hysterically.

Spencer sat up in his bed. His chest heaved as he panted for air. Sweat trickled down his face and dripped onto the floor. He swung his legs around and sat on the edge of the bed.

He heard a gentle tapping on his door. "Spence, are you alright?" It was Casey.

"I'm fine," said Spencer. "I'll be out in a minute."

He wrapped himself in a robe and stumbled into the kitchen. Casey poured a cup of coffee and set it on the table.

"Another dream?" asked Casey.

"This was a bad one," said Spencer.

"I could tell."

"Sorry if I was too loud," said Spencer. "Where's Tyler?"

Casey sat down across the table with a cup of coffee. "He went into work early today. Says he's taking you to a Tiger game tonight. He thinks you need to forget things for an evening."

Spencer rubbed his head, his hair scattering in all directions. "He might be right," he said.

Casey sipped her coffee. "So how was your trip? Did you find the old man?"

"Sure did."

"Did he know anything about Elizabeth York?"

"Not only did he know her, he was raised by her," said Spencer. "He lost his own mother on the Titanic, and Elizabeth took him under her wing. She eventually adopted him."

"I thought she died on the Titanic," said Casey.

Spencer sipped his coffee. "She was running away from an abusive husband and faked her death to throw him off the trail."

"What about the ring we saw on the news? Was that the same one she wore in the photo?"

"One and the same," said Spencer. "Before she died, she gave it to Bradley. Unfortunately, it was stolen from his house. That's how we got to see it on its way to an auction."

"Do you mean to tell me the thief is bold enough to put it on the auction block?" asked Casey.

"I thought the same thing," said Spencer. "That cop you're married to said it has probably changed hands a dozen times until the owner now has no idea it was stolen."

Casey leaned back in her chair. "So where do you go from here?" she asked. "You know that the ring was stolen and, if you listen to my husband, it was stolen years ago by your Elizabeth York. That makes the woman you love not only a thief, but dead as well. I guess I just don't understand what you're doing."

Spencer rubbed his eyes. "I wish I knew. All I know is I need to keep digging. Elizabeth York is trying to tell me something, and I believe it's of great importance."

"It must be if she's sending you a message from her grave," said Casey.

Spencer blushed. "I know how it must sound. It's like I can't help myself. Something is driving me to this. Believe me; I'd love to have my old boring life back. None of this makes sense, and it seems to be getting crazier."

Casey poured more coffee. "At first, I thought you were emotionally upset by the divorce and that's why you were imagining all this, but now I'm beginning to believe you."

A car pulled into the driveway and stopped by the backdoor. Spencer stood part way to look out the window.

"It's Gina," said Spencer. "What's she doing here?"

"Oh, I forgot to tell you," said Casey. "After you left for Memphis, I explained to her about your girlfriend and how she lived eighty years ago. Now, instead of being mad at you, she thinks you're crazy."

The door opened, and Gina stepped inside. She blushed as she first looked at Casey and then at Spencer. "Hi, Casey," she said and then turned to Spencer with a softer voice. "Hi, Spence."

Spencer nodded. "Nice to see you, Gina."

"Have a seat," said Casey. "Would you like cup of coffee?"

"No thanks," she said. "I just stopped by to apologize for the other day. Guess my temper did it to me again."

"Guess so," said Spencer.

"Casey tells me your girlfriend was on the Titanic," said Gina. "I thought it was some real person."

"She is real."

"You mean she was real. She's dead now…right?"

"I think so."

Gina scowled. "What do you mean you think so?"

"I think she's sending me messages."

Gina snickered. "Just don't let her send you a ticket for a boat ride."

Spencer turned to Casey and said nothing.

"What kind of messages is she sending?" asked Gina.

"Mostly dreams," said Spencer. "Dreams about her on a sinking ship."

"I thought most of the women and children made it. I take it your girlfriend didn't make it."

"Yeah, she made it," said Spencer. "Lived to be an old lady."

"Then, why the dreams about her on a sinking ship?" asked Gina.

Spencer slowly shook his head. "I have no idea."

Gina leaned back and sighed. "It all sounds like foolishness to me. I think you should just get on with your life."

Spencer leaned forward, his eyebrows furrowed. "I don't think you understand. I'm in love with this woman."

"She's dead, Spence!" said Gina. "You're in love with a dead woman."

"I don't think so," said Spencer.

"What do you mean you don't think so?"

"I think she's alive," said Spencer. "I saw her in a crowd."

"You saw her in a crowd," muttered Gina sarcastically. "Did you talk to her?"

"No."

"How close did you get to her?"

"Probably fifty yards."

"You saw her face to face at fifty yards."

"Not really," said Spencer. "I was looking at her from the side, but she did turn around for a moment."

"This is crazy, Spence. How can you be so sure it's her?"

Spence smiled. "I just know. Can't tell you how I know, but I just know."

Gina got to her feet and started for the door. "I was going to see if you wanted to come back home to live, but I changed my mind. I don't want some lunatic living with me."

She opened the door and turned to Casey. "If I were you, I'd kick him out of the house." With that, she slammed the door, got into her car, and drove off.

Spencer turned to Casey. "That went well, don't you think?"

 # CHAPTER SEVEN

The Detroit Tigers had been in and out of last place nearly the entire season, a position that Tiger fans had learned to accept. With such a dismal performance, premium seats were easy to come by, in fact, Spencer and his brother had been down to see them many times that season.

It was a warm summer night, and the evening breeze felt good to Spencer as he stepped up to the box office.

"Two please," said Spencer, pulling his wallet from his pocket. "And I want to be close enough to see them sweat."

"Sorry," said the man inside the booth. "All we got is upper deck left field."

"What are you talking about?" said Spencer. "Since when have you ever had a crowd to see the Tigers play?"

"Since the Yankees came to town," he said with a sneer. "Now do you want them or not?"

Spencer turned to Tyler. "They get a little snippy when they get a few people down here."

To the average person, upper deck had certain advantages. At that height, one had a commanding view of the entire field. No matter who was batting or who slid into base, nothing escaped the eyes of those seated in the upper deck. It also was a great place to catch a foul ball. People sitting on the lower decks were certainly protected from the rain, but they had less of a chance to catch a foul ball.

Holding his ticket in front of him, Spencer worked his way down the aisle until he was at the row closest to the railing. They excused themselves and edged by several people until they found their seats.

"Hey, this ain't so bad," said Spencer.

"Ain't so bad?" said Tyler. "I can hear the pilots talking to the airport, for Christ's sakes."

"Ya gotta admit, we can see everything that's going on."

"Spence, the players are taller on my big screen TV."

Spencer turned and smiled. "Thanks, Tyler."

"For what?"

"I needed to get away and clear my head."

Tyler placed his hand on Spencer's shoulder. "This thing has really got to you, hasn't it?"

"Yeah…yeah, more than I thought possible."

"What are you after?" asked Tyler. "Is it the ring, or are you after the woman?"

"I think I'm after the ring, hoping it will lead me to Elizabeth," said Spencer.

"But you know she's been gone for years now," said Tyler. "Even if she were alive, I don't think she'd look the same as she did in that photo."

"Something is happening to me, Tyler. Something I can't explain. It's as if I'm being used by some strange force."

"Do you think you're being controlled by a ghost?"

"I don't think it's trying to control me," said Spencer. "I think it's trying to tell me something."

"Do you think it's Elizabeth?"

"I'm sure of it," said Spence. "She even showed herself to me that time at the Titanic exhibit."

Tyler smiled. "Spence, my beloved brother, I'll grant you one thing, this has all been mighty strange. Those two identical pictures with the hand showing in one and not in the other was enough for me, but I have to draw the line at your seeing her alive. People just don't reappear after being dead."

"I know how it must sound," asked Spencer, "but what else can it be?"

"You were quite a long distance from her," said Tyler. "Could it have been someone who looks like her?"

"I don't know anymore. It happened so fast, and I only got a quick look at her," said Spencer. He lowered his head and ran his fingers through his hair. "Guess I could have been seeing things, but I don't think so."

"Tell you what," said Tyler, "you see her again, and I'll arrest her for impersonating a live person."

Spencer smiled. "You sure are a smart ass."

Tyler turned back to the game. "That's what they tell me."

+++

It was the last out before the seventh inning. The Tiger hitter went down swinging, and Spencer got to his feet for the seventh inning stretch. Tyler was still seated, recording the strike out in his program when he heard Spencer cry out, "There she is!"

Tyler looked up to find Spencer pointing. He sprang to his feet.

"Where?" he asked.

"She disappeared down the tunnel on that lower level," said Spencer. "She must be going to the restroom or to get a hotdog." He began to edge his way past the others in the row. "I have to find her."

"Wait for me," said Tyler, falling in behind his brother.

By the time they hit the aisle, there was a mass of people moving down the tunnel towards the concessions. They made their way through the crowds descending the steps to the lower levels.

"Is this the right level?" asked Tyler.

Spencer fought his way through the people and out of the tunnel. He looked up at the spot where they were sitting. "This is it," said Spencer. "This is the tunnel she went in."

They turned back down the tunnel and stood in the middle of the concession area. Spencer scanned the lines of people standing at each booth.

"I don't see her," he said.

Tyler turned to the restrooms. "Maybe she went to take a squirt," he said. "I wonder if dead people do nasty things like that."

Spencer ignored his brother's remark and made his way over to the ladies' restroom. He stopped just outside the door where he could watch women coming and going.

"You know you stand here for very long, and I'll have to arrest you for some perverted reason," said Tyler.

Spencer had his hands on his hips, shifting his weight from one foot to the other. "Just wait 'til you see her," said Spencer. "You'll soon see why I'm so screwed up."

Tyler grabbed him by the arm. "If you don't get away from that door, one of these women is going to call security."

By now, Spencer was breathing heavy. He studied every woman going in and coming out of the restroom.

"Maybe she wasn't hungry or had to use the restroom," said Tyler. "Maybe she was going home."

Spencer turned to the massive corridor that circled the field and led to the exits. His eyes searched the crowds until he caught a glimpse of a woman dressed in white with long-flowing hair. "There she is," he said and started in her direction.

"Dear God," muttered Tyler and fell in behind.

The game had resumed, and people were beginning to find their way back to their seats. Spencer tried to keep an eye on the woman as he wove his way through the crowds. He was gaining on her. He could tell that. She was about fifty yards away when he first saw her, and now she was at least twenty yards closer.

Without realizing it, Spencer accidentally bumped into an older woman carrying popcorn and a soft drink. The popcorn flew all over the floor, and the coke spilled onto a young boy who was in front of her. By the time he finished apologizing, he looked up and could no longer find her. He hurried to where he last saw her. There was an exit. He glanced down the tunnel that led to the outside in time to see a woman in a white dress close the back door of a yellow cab. He ran down the ramp shouting," Stop! Stop!" but he was too late. The cab slipped into the night, leaving a young man standing at the curb.

 # CHAPTER EIGHT

Charlie Stenger snapped on the light over his desk. It was after eight in the morning, and his partner, Jim Hastings, was not at work. It had been a week since Charlie had been transferred to Records and not once did he show up before Jim. He took his seat and opened a file that was on his desk. He had just turned on his computer when he heard footsteps coming down the stairs. They were slow and deliberate steps possibly made by someone who was overweight.

The door swung open and in walked Jim. He was panting profusely. "Morning, Charlie," he muttered and fell into his chair.

"You okay?" asked Charlie.

Jim took in a deep breath. "Those stairs are killing me or rather the extra sausage on the large pizzas are doing it."

"I know it's known of my business, but have you been to a doctor lately?" asked Charlie.

"I hate doctors," said Jim. "They all think the answer to every problem is to lose some weight."

"It would certainly make the trips up and down those stairs easier," said Charlie. "Besides, you might get a girlfriend if you dropped a ton or two."

Jim sneered. "I got something that might help you find the jewelry."

Charlie closed the file on his desk. "What is it?"

"My neighbor is a Titanic nut. I was talking to him last night, and he told me if you want to know anything about the Titanic to come see him."

"There are a lot of people who are into the Titanic," said Charlie. "What makes him so special?"

"He knows the names of every passenger and what happened to them," said Jim. "Know anybody else who can tell you that kind of stuff?"

Charlie paused. "Maybe I'll stop over after work."

"Give me a head start, we'll grab a couple beers from my place and I'll introduce you."

"Sounds great!" said Charlie.

+++

Jim lived in an apartment building built in the 1950's for low-income tenants. It was nestled between an auto junkyard on one side and a refinery on the other. Weeds grew wildly around the building and what little paint was left from the structure lay in small piles on the ground next to it.

Jim tapped on the rusted metal door. It swung open, and an old man stood in the doorway wearing nothing but a tattered robe loosely cinched at the waist. His face was wrinkled, and he bent over at the waist. The few strands of white hair left on his head were tossed and his face was covered with three-day stubble.

"Woodrow, this is the guy I was telling you about," said Jim cautiously stepping inside.

Charlie thrust out his hand. "My name is Charlie."

The old man ignored the extended hand and opened the door even wider. "Come on in," he said.

Charlie stepped inside. The room was dark and reeked of urine. As they ventured further inside, a dozen or so cats scrambled from the sofa. Woodrow turned on a lamp. Charlie could see cat hair drifting in and out of the light. They sat down on the sofa sending a cloud of hair into the air.

Charlie waved his hand in the air. "I can tell you like animals."

"I hate the God damn things," said Woodrow. "Two years ago, my son asked me to watch his two cats. Said they were from the same litter, and yet they made all these. Sounds a little perverted, doesn't it?"

Charlie grinned. "Well, I guess…"

"You'd think they would be born with one eye and five legs."

Charlie glanced at Jim. "I hear you're an expert on the Titanic," said Charlie.

"Well, I know more about the Titanic than how to keep cats from breeding."

"I have reason to believe some jewelry was stolen on the Titanic," said Charlie. "I was wondering if you'd know anything about such a thing?"

Woodrow fell silent. He turned to Charlie and smiled. "Life can sure be strange sometimes, can't it?"

"Well, I suppose…"

"Last month, an old friend of mine died," said Woodrow, "knew him all my life. In fact, we played together as kids. He owned something I always wanted." He took a manila envelope from his desk and handed it to Charlie. "Open it up."

Charlie opened it and withdrew a tattered, yellow piece of paper.

"His father was a policeman in England, or 'bobby' as they call them over there. The day before the Titanic went down, he got a telegram from security people on board the Titanic asking him to check out the background of a young woman and get back to them." Woodrow pointed at the paper. "You're holding that telegram."

"He saved it after all these years?" asked Charlie.

"The very next day the Titanic went down. At first, he thought whoever it was they wanted checked out might have been responsible. He figured he had hard evidence as to who might have done it. When it came out that it was an iceberg, he decided to save it anyhow probably as a souvenir."

Charlie read through the document. "Who was Elizabeth York?"

"Not much is known about Elizabeth York," said Woodrow. "Can't seem to find a thing about her prior to her short trip on the Titanic."

"Sounds like you've done some research on her," said Jim.

"Curiosity, I guess," said Woodrow. "Couldn't help but wonder why security would be interested in such a pretty girl. She didn't look all that sinister to me, but they tell me Ma Barker looked like a sweetheart herself."

"But she did die on the Titanic," said Charlie.

"That's what the official records say."

"You say that like you don't believe it."

"Let's just say I'm not at all sure what happened to her. She has no past that we can account for, and the police were interested in her. She obviously has something to hide and what better way to do it than to fake her death on the Titanic? Presumed to be dead, she now had the freedom to change her identity and move on."

"What do you think she's hiding?" asked Charlie.

"No way of knowing," said Woodrow. "Maybe she's the one who stole the jewelry you talked about."

Charlie stood. "Woodrow, it's been a pleasure. You've been a great help."

"Hope you find your jewelry," said Woodrow.

Charlie walked over to the door with Jim following right behind.

"Thanks, Woodrow, for the information," said Jim as he followed Charlie out the door.

Once outside, Jim turned to Charlie. "So, what happens now?"

Charlie smiled and smacked his hands together. "Now I go see the Luigi brothers. Frank and Melvin Luigi are both nut cases, but they can find anybody. They could find Jimmy Hoffa if someone asked them."

"Why do you call them nut cases?" asked Jim.

"They're obsessed with death," said Charlie. "Hell, they even have their own electric chair that they built right in their living room. Not sure if they've ever used it."

"Well, let's go see 'em," said Jim.

"What do you mean by let's?"

"You can't leave me behind now. We've come too far with this."

Charlie grimaces. "All right. Let's go see the Luigi brothers."

 # Chapter Nine

Frank and Melvin Luigi lived in a small house at the outskirts of town. They weren't always together. In fact, after graduating from high school, Melvin got a job as an usher at the Palace Theater. He was there for ten years and during that time lived at home with his mother.

Frank, on the other hand, tried going to college, but failed the first quarter three times before finally giving up. He was married three times and divorced three times, the third one lasting only two months. He tried working in a factory, in a department store, as a waiter, and eventually applied for and received a license to become a private investigator. He struggled for years living from time to time back home with his brother and mother, until Melvin came to work with him. From that point on, business began to take off. They soon had enough money to buy the house next to their mother and finally moved out.

Charlie had known the Luigi brothers since high school. Frank had always wanted Charlie to become his partner, and when Charlie started working for Mutual Insurance, Frank vowed never to speak to him again. As fate would have it, within two weeks, Frank needed a loan and all was forgiven.

It was early afternoon when Charlie stopped in front of their house. It was quiet in the neighborhood, and Charlie could see nobody around.

Charlie got out of the car. "Now don't forget, these guys are crazy."

Jim got out and followed behind. "Yeah, that's what you told me."

"I don't think you understand," said Charlie, stepping onto the front porch. "They should be locked up kind of crazy." He knocked on the door. "Just be careful."

They could hear the sound of locks being released, and then the door opened slightly.

"Who is it?" came a voice from with inside.

"It's Charlie...Charlie Stenger for Christ's sakes. Open the door."

"Who's that other man with you?"

"This is Jim. He's my friend, now open the god damn door!"

The door swung open just enough to enter.

"Can't be too careful," said Frank. "Lots of bad guys out there."

Charlie and Jim stepped cautiously inside. "I thought that's what you and Melvin were."

"We ain't no bad guys, Charlie," said Frank. "Hey, you're breaking my heart here with talk like that."

Frank was in his mid-thirties, short and skinny, and wore a black suit with the jacket buttoned and a felt hat on his head.

"Jesus, Frank, you look like Humphry Bogart," said Charlie. "Do you ever take that hat off?"

Frank turned and looked out the window.

"Expecting someone?" asked Charlie.

"You can never be too careful, Charlie. Know what I mean?"

Charlie glanced at the sofa. "Mind if we sit down?"

Frank pointed at a wooden chair in the corner. "Charlie, have you seen my electric chair? We built it ourselves, you know."

"Yeah, I saw it the last time I was here."

"That's right! You did see it, but as I recall you wouldn't sit in it," said Frank. "Come on, Charlie. Today's the day."

"I'm not sittin' in an electric chair," said Charlie.

"It's not plugged in."

"I don't care. That just ain't natural. Besides, it looks uncomfortable."

"I didn't make it for watching TV, for God's sakes. Now sit in it."

Charlie said nothing.

"I won't help you until you do."

Charlie paused. "Oh, all right," he said, walking over to the chair. "I don't know why I ever come over here. You guys are as crazy as loons."

He eased himself into the chair. "This thing gives me the creeps. Does it really work?"

"Sure, it works," said Frank. "We just ain't lit anybody up yet."

From behind the chair, a door opened, and Melvin entered the room. He was nearly seven feet tall and weighed over four hundred pounds.

"No wonder this thing doesn't work," said Melvin. "It's unplugged."

Charlie jumped out of the chair.

Both Frank and Melvin began to laugh hysterically.

"I don't know why I ever come over here," said Charlie, taking a seat on the sofa. "You're both certifiable."

"Come on, Charlie," said Frank. "Lighten up. We're just having a little fun with you."

"You guys beat all, you know it?"

"So, what's on your mind, Charlie?" asked Frank.

"Elizabeth York," said Charlie. "I want you to find out all you can about her."

"What all do you know?" asked Frank.

"She supposedly went down on the Titanic. I don't think she did. I think she stole a shit load of jewelry and disappeared."

"And you want to know who has it today."

"Our company paid out millions years ago on a claim made by some big shot from England," said Charlie.

"So, you want to get back the jewelry and give it back to the company," said Frank sarcastically.

"Never mind what I'm going to do with the stuff, just find it for me, and I'll make us both rich."

Frank turned to Melvin. He was spinning the chamber of a handgun and holding it to his head. "What about him?"

Charlie watched as Melvin pulled the trigger, saw him grimace and pull the trigger again. "Like I said…"

Frank frowned. "Melvin, will you quit playing games?"

Charlie got to his feet. "I'm out of here," he said, opened the door and walked out.

 # CHAPTER TEN

It was late morning when Casey shuffled into the kitchen. Spencer was already drinking coffee and sitting at the table with the two photos of Elizabeth York. Casey poured herself a cup and sat down across from Spencer.

"Morning, Casey," said Spencer. "Don't think I've ever seen you sleep in before. You okay?"

"Didn't feel so good last night when I went to bed, so I didn't set my alarm. I think the extra sleep did some good."

Spencer returned to the pictures. "Glad to hear it," he muttered.

"How were the dreams last night?"

"Worse than ever," said Spencer. "Did you ever dream about water bubbling from an iron grate and someone reaching out to you through the bars of the grate?"

Casey said nothing.

Spencer shook his head as if waking from a sleep. "You'd think I'd be use to it by now."

"I would hope you never get used to something like that, even if it was a dream," said Casey.

Spencer nodded his head in agreement.

A wistful smile spread across Casey's face. "Spencer, I can't help but think this whole thing is getting out of hand. Your obsession with this woman can't be healthy for you."

"Well, I can't help but agree with you there," said Spencer.

"I talked with Gina. She wants you back."

"What about her boyfriend?"

"Spence, she wants a second chance," said Casey. "She even got rid of her boyfriend."

"In other words, he dumped her, and now she's all alone."

Casey smiled. "She didn't say one way or the other, but that was my guess as well. Either way, I really think it would be best for you."

Spencer stood and walked across the room. He turned and leaned against the sink. "Maybe you're right," he said. "Maybe that would be best. I mean how sane is it to be chasing after a woman who has been dead for ninety years? I must be out of my mind. And she says she wants me back."

Casey nodded her head. "That's what she said."

Spencer returned to his chair and sat down. "You know, I don't know why this is happening to me, but it's making me crazy. Maybe that's exactly what I need, to move back home."

"You could at least try it," said Casey.

"God, I'm a sucker," said Spencer. "She takes up with another man and when it doesn't work out, she wants me back. What a loser I am!"

"She made a mistake," said Casey. "We all make mistakes."

"I must be crazy, but I'm going to do it," said Spencer. "I'm going back home."

+++

It was early afternoon when Spencer pulled into his driveway. He stopped halfway and got out of his car. It had been a long time, or at least it seemed that way. The lawn needed to be mowed, and weeds grew where once there were none.

Spencer got out of his car and walked to the front door. Seemed strange knocking on his own front door, but he knew he had to. He wondered if he was doing the right thing. Not many men would come back, not after what she did. For God's sakes, the woman went to bed with another man! It just didn't seem right to forgive such a deed. What was right and what was wrong didn't seem important right now. After all, there was that time he had a short fling with the neighbor lady, but the difference was he didn't get caught.

Spencer stepped onto the porch and before he could ring the doorbell or set down his luggage, the door opened.

"Hi," said Gina, standing in the open doorway.

"Hi," said Spencer, still holding his bags.

A few moments passed until Gina stepped aside. "Come on in," she said.

Spencer stepped inside and dropped his luggage at the front door. "The place looks great," he said, glancing around the room.

"Thanks," she said and pointed at his favorite chair, "have a seat."

He eased himself into the chair and leaned it back in a reclining position. "Damn, I forgot how comfortable this chair is."

"It always was your favorite," she said.

Spencer caressed the fabric until he noticed a dark spot on one of the arms. His smile disappeared. "Your friend smoked, didn't he?"

"Why, yes, he did," said Gina. "Why do you ask?"

"He burnt my chair," said Spencer. "It looks like the son of a bitch snubbed out a cigarette on the arm of my chair."

"I did that, Spence," she said. "I fell asleep with a lit cigarette. I'm sorry."

Anger disappeared from Spencer's face. "I can't believe you'd do that to my chair."

"I'm sorry. I really am."

Spencer glanced around the room. He was nervous and wasn't sure why. He had known Gina most of his life and yet today felt like the first time. "The place looks about the same."

"You've only been gone for less than a year."

"Yeah, but you've kept it up nice."

"Couldn't afford to make any changes living off just my salary and all," she said.

Silence fell on the room.

"So, what happened to you and your boyfriend, anyhow?" asked Spencer.

Gina began to fidget with the arm of her chair. "I kicked him out!"

"You kicked him out, or did he dump you?"

Gina stopped fidgeting and tightly gripped the chair. "You know, this sounds a lot like where we left off."

Spencer paused for a moment. "Yeah, you're right. Sorry."

"Just why did you agree to come back here, anyhow?" she asked.

"I don't know," said Spencer, "I guess because you asked me to."

Gina turned away trying to hide the look of pain on her face. "You haven't changed, have you?"

"What'd I say this time?" asked Spencer.

"I had hoped you moved back because you still had feelings for me, not because you were invited."

Spencer paused wide-eyed. "I'm not scoring many points here, am I?"

Gina said nothing.

"I'm sorry, Gina," said Spencer. "I really am. I'm being an insensitive jerk right now."

Gina sneered. "You can say that again."

"I've spent so much time around guys in the last year, I forgot how to act in the presence of a woman."

Gina sat up in her chair. "What do you mean by that?"

"Just what I said," said Spencer. "You can't talk to a woman the same as you do to a man."

"Now it's all coming back to me," said Gina, "I'd forgotten how much of a chauvinist you are. So, tell me, what do you say to your friends that you couldn't say to me?"

"Come on, Gina. You can't be serious. You're doing it right now. Everything I say you pick apart and try to start a fight over it. Women are too sensitive. They take everything personal and want to fight about it. I can call my best friend an asshole, and he wouldn't even bat an eye."

"That's because if he's a friend of yours, he already knows he's an asshole," said Gina.

Spencer got to his feet. "Well, I can see where this conversation is going." He walked across the room and opened the door. "I got shit to do. See you later."

+++

Spencer spent the rest of the day in the library researching the names of the people who survived the Titanic, as well as those who died on that fateful night. He had hoped to find something that would explain the strange events that were happening to him.

One of the more interesting names Spencer found was of his own namesake, Ellington. Harrison Ellington had booked passage on the Titanic to start a new life in the United States. He was a businessman who had spent his life trading commodities on the open market. Spencer ran out of time before he could check his genealogy to see if they were related.

It was nearly 6:00 in the evening when he knocked on Gina's door. She opened it slightly and peeked out.

"I didn't expect to see you again," she said, swinging the door open.

Spencer stepped inside. "I screwed up big time. I was wondering if I could try it again."

"Sure. Why not?" she said. "One more fight here or there doesn't make any difference."

"No more fights," said Spencer. "I promise no more. I don't want to fight with you anymore. Seems like that's all we've ever done since we've known each other."

Gina returned to the sofa. The television was on and the news was just beginning. "Can't say much for our relationship," she said.

Spencer sat next to her. "I don't know. I once read that arguments are healthy for a marriage."

"I think they're talking about an occasional argument, not a steady diet of them," she said. "Besides all that, what are you doing sitting this close to me?"

Spencer put his arm around her and smiled. "We didn't fight all the time," he said in a soft voice. "In fact, I remember some really hot times."

Gina gave him a puzzled look. "You're crazy."

"Remember our first time, when we checked into that sleazy motel? The sheets were so dirty they moved all by themselves."

Gina smiled, "And the maid walked in on us when we were…"

"Damn, I forgot about that," said Spencer. "That was embarrassing."

"You brought me carnations that day," she said. The smile disappeared from her face. "I think that was the last time you ever gave me flowers."

"I plan to change all that," he said. He leaned over and kissed her on the cheek. "I heard that you have to work at a marriage, and that's what I plan to do."

"I must be crazy, but I actually believe that you mean it this time," she said and then kissed him on the lips.

"I do mean it," he said with feeling. "I just need time to prove it."

He pulled her close and kissed her passionately. He could feel her tension and resistance draining away as she relaxed and kissed him back. It was like the old days when they were first married. The excitement and passion were back. Spencer gently ran the tips of his fingers over her breasts. She squirmed at his touch, her nipples hardened. He kissed her ear lobes and down the back of her neck. He could hear her softly panting through slightly parted lips. He grabbed her breast. He could feel her hard nipple in his hand. Gina pulled away as he began to slowly unbutton her blouse. Her chest was heaving as the passion grew within her.

As he slowly unfastened one button after the other, Spencer could hear the six o'clock edition of the news in the background, but was too distracted to hear what was being said. He had just unfastened her last button when a commercial finished and another story began. Spencer reached around to unfasten her bra when the name, Bradley McKinley caught his attention. He stopped fidgeting with the catches on her bra strap and turned to the TV.

File footage of the Titanic was shown as the newsman told the story. "The last known survivor of the Titanic was stricken with a heart attack today. Eighty-nine-year-old Bradley McKinley was just a boy at the time, on his way to America with his mother." Spencer pushed Gina away. He pointed at the television. "That's Bradley!" he shouted.

"That's who?" asked Gina with a puzzled look.

"That's Bradley McKinley, the man I met in Memphis."

She pulled her open blouse over her breasts and fastened the top two buttons. "What are you talking about?"

"He is the last known survivor of the Titanic, and I need to see him one more time."

"He just had a heart attack," said Gina. "What makes you think you can see him before he dies?"

Spencer bent over and put his shoes back on. "I don't know, but I'm off to Memphis."

"What do you mean you're off to Memphis?"

"I have to talk to him."

"You can't be serious!"

Spencer got to his feet and started for the door. "I know this is a little unusual, but I have to go."

Gina stood and pointed at him. "If you walk out that door, don't you ever come back again!"

Spencer opened the door. "I'm really sorry about this."

"I'll never speak to you again!"

"Gotta go," he said and closed the door behind him.

 # Chapter Eleven

It was five o'clock and Charlie Stenger was just getting home from work. He grabbed a beer from the refrigerator, turned on the TV, and sat down in his recliner. Today was not unlike any other day, except today was payday, and payday meant a trip to the liquor store for a six-pack and fifty dollars worth of lottery tickets.

Charlie dug a dime from his pocket and scratched it over the first ticket. "Damn!" he said as he threw the worthless ticket onto the floor. He gulped his beer and scratched another ticket. "Another loser," he muttered.

He was near the end of the tickets when he heard a knock on the door. Charlie got up and swung the door open.

Frank Luigi stared at the tickets scattered on the floor. "Are those lottery tickets?"

"Yeah," said Charlie.

"You sure know how to have a good time," said Frank.

Charlie said nothing.

Frank pushed the door open. "Well, are you going to let us in?"

Charlie stepped aside. "Did you get the information I wanted?"

The two men stepped inside. Frank took a seat, while Melvin stood beside him. "Didn't you ask us to perform a service for you? We wouldn't be here right now if we didn't complete our mission."

"Jesus, Frank, just get on with it."

"What happened to good old hospitality?" said Frank. "Time was when you had visitors, you'd offer them a drink."

"God damn it, Frank! What did you find out?"

Frank pulled a folded piece of paper from his pocket and began to read. "Elizabeth York was officially declared a casualty on the Titanic. It appears she changed her name so that everyone would think she died, then later on she married a guy named Longberry, not sure what his first name was. They adopted some young boy and had a daughter of their own by the name of Beatrice."

Charlie sat straight in his chair. "Well? What else?"

"Elizabeth York or Longberry died in a car accident. Her daughter, Beatrice, died from food poisoning, and there's no record of what happened to the adopted boy. I'm sure he's a goner, considering how old he must be."

Frank looked up from his paper and stared at Charlie.

"Go on," said Charlie.

"That's it," said Frank.

"What do you mean that's it?"

"I don't have any more."

"Did Beatrice have any kids?"

"I don't know."

"Why not?"

"The library was closing, and I had to go."

Charlie leaned back and ran his fingers through his hair. "Frank, everything you've given me so far is bullshit! All these people are dead. I want to know if this Beatrice lady had a kid. Chances are, he's the one I'm after."

"Well, the library opens tomorrow morning at…"

"I'm telling you that Elizabeth dame was as slick as they come. She stole the jewelry, made it look like she died on the Titanic, and lived happily ever after."

"What makes you think she didn't sell the stuff?" asked Frank.

"A broad like that didn't do it for the money," said Charlie. "She did it for the challenge, the adventure. Besides, females like her just want to own the stuff. They love expensive bobbles like that. Unless I miss my guess, that jewelry is still in the family."

Frank got to his feet and started for the door. "Okay, I'll find out if Beatrice squirted any kids."

"And when you do, pay 'em a visit and find out what they know," said Charlie as he turned up the volume on the TV.

"I might have to lean on 'em to get what I want."

"That's fine, now get out of here," said Charlie.

Frank opened the door. "Sure, could have used a drink."

Charlie turned over his shoulder. "Get out of here!"

 # Chapter Twelve

Spencer parked in front of his brother's house. He needed to pack some clothes before starting for Memphis. It was nearly seven o'clock, late to be knocking on someone's door, but he knew Tyler and Casey would be watching TV by now.

"Hi, Spence," said Casey, swinging the door open.

"Hi, Casey. Can I come in?"

"Sure. I thought you were moving back with Gina."

Spencer stepped inside. "Something's come up."

Tyler walked into the room. "What's up, Spence?"

"Old man McKinley, the last survivor of the Titanic, just had a heart attack and I'm on my way to see him. Just needed a few things."

"What about Gina," asked Casey, "how's she taking this?"

Spencer rolled his eyes. "Mentioned something about if you walk through that door or something like that."

"Spence, I know this means a lot to you," asked Casey, "but are you sure you want to sacrifice a chance to get back together with Gina?"

"Stay out of it, Casey," said Tyler. "The boy knows what he's doing."

"That's just it," said Spencer. "I really don't know what I'm doing. It seems like I just get deeper and deeper into this thing, and I don't know why. I should get on with my life. I mean look at me. I'm pathetic. Divorced, no job, and I'm chasing after a woman who died eons ago."

"You know I'll be the first to encourage someone who is in love, but this is different," said Casey. "This is kinda sick."

"It's not sick!" said Tyler, sliding to the edge of his chair. Both Spencer and Casey turned. "If you don't do this thing, Spence, you'll regret it all your life. You'll always wonder what if, and you'll have enough of those what ifs in your life." He paused. Spencer smiled. "So, as they say, follow that dream. Take it where it leads you. You only live once and all that stuff."

Spencer's serious face turned into a grin. "You really think I should?"

"I really think you should," said Tyler. "I don't know what you're doing, but I think you should do it anyhow."

Spencer jumped to his feet. "I'll do it. First, I'm going to Memphis."

"Oh, Spence, I forgot," said Casey. "The nursing home called and said your great grandpa Harrison has been asking for you."

"That's impossible," said Spencer. "He's been out of his head for years. I really don't have time for this."

"Sure, ignore the man," said Tyler. "He's only ninety-nine years old, has been delirious for years, and yet he asked for you. Don't forget, he's the guy who made sure we had presents for Christmas."

"You don't play fair," said Spencer. "Okay, I'll go to see him before I go to Memphis."

Harrison Ellington had been admitted into the nursing home nearly twenty years ago. It wasn't because he was an invalid or helpless. Something happened to Harrison that seemed to end his life long before his body died. For years he avoided family and friends, until he eventually locked himself away from the world. A recluse by choice, his body soon withered, and the light in his eyes disappeared.

The marriage he entered soon ended, doomed to unhappiness from the start. A son was born and prospered, but the Second World War claimed him as a casualty. Harrison mourned his loss, but it was more than that. Something had poisoned him, poisoned the very soul and spirit of the man.

As the years passed, the rest of the family became less concerned and eventually considered him to be a dark family secret. No one in the family spoke of Harrison Ellington without whispering.

A heart attack nearly took his life and led to his admittance into a nursing home. For the next twenty years, he lived in quiet desperation. Forced to live in the company of others, Harrison considered his privacy compromised and his life without meaning. Visits by the family soon diminished to a quick stop at Christmas, until today when a family member was actually summoned.

Spencer wove his way down the hallway past the zombie-like residents. Some wandered down the hall while most sat in wheelchairs along the walls. At the end of one of the halls, Spencer turned into a room. Harrison was lying on his back his legs thrashing and his arms flailing in all directions.

"We'll see about that!" he shouted. "That kind of conduct will come to an end on my watch!"

A young woman dressed in white had just finished feeding him and was cleaning him.

Spencer stepped closer. "Hi, my name is Spencer."

"So, you're Spencer," she said, starting for the door. "He's been in a stew waiting for you."

"I heard he asked for me."

"Never seen anything like it," she said. "The man has done nothing but talk gibberish for the five years I've been here, and yet he sat straight up in bed and asked for you."

"Is he okay?"

"What's okay with a man who pees his pants and can't count to three," she said. "Physically, he ain't too bad for a man nearly a century old, but mentally, he's a houseplant." She paused at the open doorway. "Talk to him. Hopefully, you didn't make a trip out here for nothing."

Spencer edged closer. "Hi, Grandpa."

"Time waits for no man!" he said with a loud voice. "We'll march to our grave with dignity. I won't crawl to my destiny like some form of lower life."

Spencer stepped to the side of his bed. He seemed out of control. His eyes were blurred and seemed unable to focus on anything. "Grandpa, it's me, Spence. You asked for me."

"Over the top, boys," he said, his head rolling from side-to-side. "Let the wounded fend for themselves."

Spencer leaned over and brushed the few white strands of hair from his eyes. His face was tired and weathered, his eyes cold. Spencer listened to the old man babble when suddenly he reached up and grabbed Spencer by the arm. His body stopped moving, his eyes fixed on Spencer's eyes.

"I know what you're going through...the dreams, the desires. She haunted me, too. God, did she get to me," said Harrison.

"Grandpa, what woman?"

The old man released his grip on Spencer's arm and laid back down. "She was the most beautiful woman in the world, and yet her beauty ruined my life. That's why you need to go and find her. She was a duchess, you know. Duchess of Devonshire. You must promise me you will find her. Don't let her slip away like I did."

Spencer leaned forward. "Who are you talking about, Grandpa?"

"Your dreams, Spencer. Trust in your dreams. She comes to you every night."

Spencer pulled a folded picture from his pocket and opened it. "Is this the woman?" he asked, holding the photo in front of Harrison.

From the moment the old man saw the photo, Spencer knew. He knew that this old man who had been delirious for years was now speaking to him with a clear mind.

Harrison smiled. It was a smile of complete contentment. His tense body seemed to relax as he studied the picture. Then he looked into Spencer's eyes. It was a plaintive look, one that would haunt Spencer for the rest of his life. It was as if all the sorrow in his life that was buried deep within his soul, surfaced at that moment.

"Sometimes in life you wonder if you've done the right thing," said Harrison. "Life is a journey, and along that journey, we make decisions, forks in the road if you prefer. I chose a path a long time ago. It seemed like the right thing to do, but how could the right thing cause so much misery?"

Spencer leaned closer. "What was this thing you did, Grandpa? What was it that caused you so much misery?"

Harrison began to breathe in short gasps. "You're at that fork in the road, Spencer. Don't make the same mistake I made."

"What mistake, Grandpa? What mistake?"

Harrison stiffened. His eyes widened as he grabbed his chest.

"Something's wrong," said Spencer. "I need to get help."

He started to leave when Harrison grabbed him by the shirt and pulled him closer. His face was now inches from Harrison. "Never mind about that, son. There's nothing they can do. Before I go, I have one more thing to tell you."

"Go?" said Spencer. "Don't talk like that, Grandpa. "You're going to live for…"

Harrison passed a set of keys into Spencer's hand. "One of those keys is for my house." He coughed violently. Blood trickled from his mouth. "In my closet is a box, and in that box are letters. You must get them before they get into the wrong hands."

"What do you want me to do with them?"

"After I'm gone, tear them up, burn them, whatever you have to do to destroy them," said Harrison.

"Why, Grandpa? Why do you want me to destroy them?"

Harrison pulled even harder on his shirt. His eyebrows furrowed, his face determined. "Promise me you'll do this thing for me. Promise me."

"Yeah, sure Grandpa," said Spencer. "I'll destroy them if that's what you want."

Harrison released his grip on Spencer's shirt and settled back down in his bed. "They must die with me."

Spencer glanced at the keys in his hand. "What about this other key, Grandpa? What does it go to?"

Harrison began to cough again, his breathing in short gasps. "That key unlocks a box that is with the letters."

"What's in the box, Grandpa?" asked Spencer.

Slowly, the old man began to relax. "You'd better go now," he said. "I need to sleep."

+++

It was over an hour later that Spencer stopped in front of his brother's house. He walked to the front of the house and knocked on the door.

"What are you doing here?" asked Tyler. "I figured you to be halfway to Memphis."

Spencer said nothing. The sober look on his face said it all.

"Let me guess," said Tyler. "Grandpa Harrison died."

"No, but he won't last much longer," said Spencer.

"Sorry to hear it," said Tyler. "Come on in and sit down."

"I really don't have the time," said Spencer. "I wonder if you could go with me over to Grandpa's house?"

"Sure. Why?"

"Grandpa gave me the key to his house and wanted me to get a box of letters. I would rather have someone with me when I do it."

Tyler opened the door. "I've always wanted to see inside that house. Let's go."

+++

Harrison Ellington had lived at the corner of Ludington and Dover Streets nearly all his life. It was a two-story Victorian home built in the late 1800's, originally owned by a doctor who lived in it for over twenty years and then sold it to Hiram Ellington, Harrison's father. Harrison was born there, and when his parents died when he was eighteen he continued to live in that old majestic house for the rest of his life.

In the early years, Harrison spent his spare time with the upkeep and maintenance of the house inside and out. His lawn was spotless and manicured to perfection, not only the front and sides, but the back as well. In the back of the house was a prize rose garden while daffodils, marigolds, and petunias lined the walks around the house.

But that all changed. Everyone in town saw it happening. The once pristine estate was decaying before their very eyes. Small piles of dried paint lay in the weeds around the perimeter of the house, and the rose garden withered and died. Gone was the ivy that adorned the front entrance to the house, and throughout the grounds grew weeds where once there were none.

Spencer stopped in front of the house. They got out of the car and walked to the front door.

"What's that smell?" asked Spencer.

Tyler stopped and glanced at the outside of the house. The only paint remaining was a few faded white specks. "That's rotting wood," he said. "I'd say the place is about to fall down."

"What a shame," said Spencer. "It looks like this was quite a place in its time."

They opened the front door and stepped inside. It was just as they had imagined and more. High arched ceilings seem to disappear into the darkness. The floors were covered with floral pattern carpeting, and the walls were made of dark stained oak. Generations of spiders had left undisturbed networks of webs throughout the house.

Spencer moved cautiously into the dining room. "D'ya suppose the Munsters live here?"

Tyler smiled. "I'm carrying a gun, and I'm scared."

"What do you suppose he did all day in this place?" Spencer asked. "They say he never went anyplace. He even had his groceries delivered."

"I don't think I want to know," said Tyler. "He was one messed up guy."

Spencer started for the staircase. "We need to go upstairs to find his room."

"Oh, I don't think so," said Tyler. "I think there's some kind of law about going into an old person's bedroom. At least, it doesn't sound any too healthy."

Spencer stopped at the top of the stairs and gazed down the hallway. There were doors leading to six bedrooms, a bathroom and three linen closets. "Wonder which one is his."

"Try the one at the end of the hallway. That should be the master bedroom."

Spencer walked to the end of the hall and slowly opened the door. It groaned in protest. "What a bedroom," he said. It was a huge room with windows that extended from the floor to the ceiling. A large canopy bed sat in the middle with two fireplaces one at either end.

Spencer opened a closet door. It had cedar-lined walls to keep the wool-eating insects out. On the floor at one end was a cardboard box, partially hidden by a stack of old newspapers. He picked it up, carried it into the bedroom and set it on the bed. They both stared at the box.

"Grandpa asked me to destroy these letters, I'm sure he meant for us not to read them," said Spencer.

"You're not going to destroy these without taking a look, are you?" asked Tyler.

"I don't think we should betray Grandpa's wishes."

Tyler pulled the tape from the top of the box and opened the flaps. "Damn! What a shit load of letters!"

The box contained hundreds of letters nearly all of them still within their envelopes. Spencer picked up one that was spread open on top of the pile.

"This one's written to Grandpa," said Spencer. He paused as he read the first page. "Kinda mushy stuff."

"They all look like love letters, and they're from the same girl," said Tyler. "Old Grandpa was some kind of a lady's man."

Spencer was still reading. "Who is the lucky girl, anyway?"

Tyler picked up a letter still in the envelope. "The return address is faded," he said bringing it closer. "Hey, wait a second. What was the name of that chick you've had the hots for, the one who supposedly went down with the Titanic?"

"Elizabeth York. Why?"

"She was the one writing all these letter to Grandpa."

Spencer picked up one of the envelopes and studied the return address. "It must be a mistake." He rifled through the box picking up letter after letter. He looked up in disbelief. "It can't be."

Tyler smiled. "Oh, I think it can."

"Maybe it's another Elizabeth York."

"What if it isn't? What if it's your Elizabeth York?"

"Did you notice the return address?" Spencer asked. "She sent them from here. She must have been living in this house."

"Did you notice where she was sending them?" Tyler asked. "She was sending them to Grandpa, but he was in England. Now go figure that." He dropped a letter back into the box. "You got yourself a real mystery here."

Spencer returned the letter and closed the box. "Sorry, Grandpa. I know I promised to destroy these letters, but not just yet. There are just too many unanswered questions here."

Tyler grinned. "Yeah, like what's he doing with your gal?"

Spencer scooped up the box and started for the door. "Thanks for coming over with me."

"You know, you owe me for more than just that," said Tyler.

Spencer opened the door. "Gotta go. See ya."

+ + +

It was early afternoon when Spencer pulled into Memphis. He was tired from the long trip and decided to check into a motel near the hospital. The exit he wanted was just a mile ahead, so he slowed his car and eased into the right lane. Just before he reached the off ramp, a woman driving a black BMW pulled across three lanes of traffic and cut close enough in front of him he had to hit the brakes.

"Bitch!" he screamed out the window then followed her as she changed lanes and entered another interstate highway. As they merged into the traffic, Spencer accelerated and pulled alongside of her. He tried to see into the car, but the windows were covered in a dark tint. He flipped his middle finger in her direction in spite of the fact he could not see her reaction. Before he could even lower his hand, she hit the gas and pulled away from him at a tremendous speed.

Spencer soon forgot about the woman in the black BMW and was looking for his next exit when he saw the car stopped on the roadside with the hood propped open. A tall, slender woman was bent over with her head under the hood. She was wearing a long black dress with high heels. For a moment he considered leaving her stranded along the roadside, but chivalry soon prevailed, and he pulled over in front of her. He was nearly fifty yards in front of her when his car came to a stop. As he got out of his car, he noticed she had slipped back into her own car and locked the doors.

Spencer stopped in front of the car. Steam trickled from the engine. He moved around to the side of the car. "Hey, lady. Looks like you could use some help."

She said nothing.

Spencer leaned over and peered through the glass. He could see her outline. "I know we had a little road rage thing back there, but I'm not upset. I just thought you might need some help."

He could see her turn in his direction. "Go away!" she said.

"Hey lady, it's no skin off my nose if you sit here until you rot. I just thought you might like some help. I'm no stranger to the mechanical operation of a motor vehicle and might just be able to get you back on the road, but I need your permission first."

"Anyone who is as rude of a driver as you are has to be dangerous," she said. "Now go away before I call the police."

Spencer stood straight. "Rude! Who are you calling rude? You're the one who cut me off in the first place. You nearly ran into me and you call me rude!"

He waited for a response, but she said nothing.

"Where did you get your driver's license anyhow, Woolworth's?" said Spencer. "Why I bothered to stop, I'll never know. This is what you get when you try to be a Good Samaritan."

"Please leave," she said. "I don't want your help."

"All right for you, lady," said Spencer. "Don't forget I tried to help. The next guy or guys who stop might not have your best interest at heart." He paused for a moment. "The only reason I stopped in the first place is I have a mother and I would hope someone would help her if she needed it."

She still said nothing.

Spencer turned and started for his car. "That's it! I've had enough! I really don't need this. In fact, I'm late already."

The window on the driver's side rolled down a crack.

"Sir!" she called out. Spencer stopped. "Do you think you can fix my car?"

He turned around. "If man built it, I can fix it," he said proudly.

"Then you have my permission to fix it," she said from inside the vehicle.

Spencer rolled his eyes. "I feel so honored," he muttered.

He walked over to the side of the car and leaned over the motor. He tugged and pulled on the sparkplug wires and fuel line then checked the air filter. Everything seemed normal.

"Did you find the problem?" she yelled from the window.

"Not yet," he answered.

Spencer stood straight and studied the engine. He remembered watching a mechanic years ago as he tried to solve the same problem. He leaned back over and disconnected a sparkplug wire. Spencer wasn't quite sure why he did that, but he guessed that it was to determine if there was electricity flowing to the plug.

He held the cap near the end of the plug and shouted, "Turn 'er over for me."

She turned the key and the starter whirled. Spencer could see a spark gapping from the cap to the plug.

Then it happened. While she was cranking the starter, the fuel line burst spewing gasoline all over the hot engine and the exposed plug wire in Spencer's hand. Almost immediately, the gasoline ignited. Fire swept across the engine. In seconds, fire was leaping in the air, smoke billowing from the engine compartment.

Spencer stepped back. He turned to the woman inside the car. "Get the hell out of there! She's going to explode!" He waited long enough to see the driver's door open and then dove for the ditch on the other side of the road. He looked up in time to see a woman rolling down the side of the ditch, landing on her back. Her legs were straight up in the air and her dress was at her waist. She quickly turned over and pulled her dress over her legs.

They both stared quietly at the inferno that was once her car. She slowly turned to Spencer. "You did that on purpose!"

Spencer turned in her direction. She was wearing sunglasses, but looked strangely familiar. "I did what?"

"You torched my car to get back at me, didn't you?"

On his knees, he inched closer to her. He glared at her face trying to imagine what she looked like without the sunglasses. "It was an accident, I tell you."

She got to her feet and brushed off her clothes. "That was no accident. You're just an evil man."

Spencer glanced at the burning car. Flames were leaping high in the air. He turned back to the woman beside him. "I know this isn't the best time to ask this, but could you take off your sunglasses for a minute?"

"What did you just say?" she asked.

"I was wondering if you might remove your sunglasses. You see, you look just like…"

"You just destroyed my eighty-thousand-dollar vehicle, and you want me take off my sunglasses? Are you crazy?"

"You look like someone I know or rather someone I'd like to know. That didn't sound right either. I've been trying to find you because you look like someone who has been dead for a long time."

"What?"

"I'm not winning many points with you, am I?"

"Leave!" she said.

"Huh?"

"Just get out of here. I don't want you near me or my burning car."

"Don't you want a ride somewhere?"

"The police will soon be here, and I'll get a ride with them, now get out of here."

Spencer got to his feet. "What about the sunglasses? You wouldn't, by any chance, let me…"

She pointed at his car. "Go! Get out of here!"

By the time Spencer pulled away, he could see fire trucks and police cars in his rear-view mirror. He felt bad leaving her there, but he also was sure she wanted him to go.

Spencer checked into a motel only two blocks from the hospital. It had been a long trip and he was tired, so he lay on the bed and took a nap. Four hours later, he awoke to the sound of the dumpster just outside his window being emptied. He jumped out of bed and started for the bathroom. After a quick shower and a change of clothes, he was off to the hospital.

The lights on the fourth floor were dimmed, and it was quiet as a tomb. The residents on this floor were older and in recovery. Spencer stopped at the end of the hall and turned into Room 423. He could see Bradley lying in his bed and a woman standing beside him with her back to Spencer. He quietly stepped inside the doorway. Bradley turned to him and smiled.

"Hey, Spencer," he said with a smile. "How ya doing?"

The woman turned around. It was she! Elizabeth York! It wasn't possible! How could a woman who died on the Titanic be here looking the same as she did all those years ago?

Spencer stepped closer. He stared in disbelief.

"It's you!" she said, her face scowled. "What are you doing here? Never mind what you're doing here, just get out of here!"

"Madison, Madison, what's the matter here?" Bradley asked.

She turned to Bradley. "Do you know this man?"

"Yes, I do," he replied. "Do you?"

"This man set my car on fire!"

Bradley smiled. "He did what?"

Spencer stepped forward. He was still staring at Madison. "You're Elizabeth York, the woman in the photograph." He turned to Bradley. "You remember! This is the woman standing on the deck of the Titanic! You made me a copy of the picture."

Bradley chuckled. "Spencer, I'd like you to meet my great niece, Madison Riley. Madison, this is Spencer...I don't recall your last name."

"Ellington," he said, extending his hand, "Spencer Ellington."

She glanced down at his open hand and turned away. "I don't care what your name is, just go away."

"Madison, that's no way to treat a guest," said Bradley. "Now the man has come a long way to see me. Let him in."

Madison lightly stomped her foot. "I'll tell you what. You go ahead, and I'll wait out in the hall until you're done. And I'm only doing this because of Uncle Bradley."

They watched as she marched out of the room.

"That went well, I think," said Bradley.

"That's the girl of my dreams," said Spencer.

"I don't think she shares the same enthusiasm for you."

"I kinda got off on the wrong foot."

"So, it would seem."

Spencer paused. "That's it! The girl of my dreams! Here all along I thought I was dreaming about Elizabeth York, and all the time it was Madison Riley!"

"But you didn't know Madison before today," said Bradley.

"That tells me that Elizabeth York has been leading me to her."

"I'll say this much for you, sonny, you sure have an imagination."

"At least, I don't have to feel so crazy anymore," said Spencer. "At least, I'm chasing a real live woman instead of one who has been dead for years."

"Oh, she's really alive," said Bradley. "What you got there ain't no ordinary filly. She's got more spunk than a bronco."

"Is she married?"

"Just got divorced from some guy who claims to be a billionaire," said Bradley. "He might have been for all I know. I'm just glad she dumped him."

"I know I shouldn't ask this, but do you think I have a chance with her?"

"Spence, my boy, she's never been tamed. She's got a free spirit like nobody you ever met. If it's a stay-at-home wife you're looking for, she's not the one for you. She started her own cosmetic business that did over ten million dollars last year."

"And I don't even have a job," muttered Spencer.

"Then all I can say is good luck, my little buckaroo. 'Cause you're going to need it."

Spencer glanced at the floor. "I had all these questions, and now I can't think of a one."

"I'll tell you what," said Bradley. "Why don't you slip outside while I talk with Madison. Then I want to talk with both of you together."

"Sure thing," said Spencer and opened the door.

Madison was leaning against the wall with her arms folded.

"He wants to see you," said Spencer. She started for the door. "Then he wants to see both of us." She kept on walking as if she didn't hear the last statement.

"He seems like a nice young man," said Bradley.

"So did Hitler," said Madison.

"I guess burning up your car is not the best way to start a new relationship, but I want you to do me a favor."

"Oh, don't do this to me, Uncle Bradley."

"I just want you to give him a chance."

"Why should I? He torched my car. I don't like him. He's ugly. He even flipped me off."

"You two have a lot in common, more than you know. Besides, it's a dying man's request. Nobody with a heart can turn down a dying man's request."

"You're not playing fair," said Madison.

"There is no such thing as playing fair when it comes to matters of the heart."

"Okay, so I give him another chance and I still don't like him, then can I tell him to get lost?"

"It's a deal."

Madison relaxed. "So, when are you going to get out of here and come home?" she asked.

Bradley placed his hand on top of hers. "That's just it, Madison. I'm not coming home."

"What do you mean you're not coming home? You know I've told you before, you're only as old as you…"

"It's my time, Madison. Somehow I just know it."

"Uncle Bradley, please don't talk like that."

"You and I have always told each other the truth, and I won't lie to you now. This old body is just worn out."

Madison gripped his hand. "But you always said you'd live to a hundred."

Bradley smiled. "Hey, I gave it a heck of a try. Besides, I had a great life, had some fun along the way. Who knows? Maybe the afterlife will be even more fun."

A tear streaked down Madison's cheek. "Seems funny. I feel closer to you in some ways than I did my own parents."

"I fell in love with you the day you were born," said Bradley. "I don't know why. You weren't my own. Yet, I felt a love for you as if you were my very own."

"It does seem funny now that you mention it," said Madison. "Uncles are someone you see on Thanksgiving Day, and yet here you are, my great uncle, and I feel as close to you as if you were my own father."

"It's for that very reason that I need to talk to you and that young man out there in the hall."

Madison stiffened. "What does he have to do with all this, Uncle Bradley?"

The old man struggled to sit up in bed. "That young man out there has a lot to do with this, more than you know, and even more than he knows."

"I don't think I've ever known you to be quite so mysterious, Uncle Bradley. It's just too bad it has to be with that...that idiot."

Bradley pointed at the door. "Why don't you ask him to come in here?"

"Do I have to?"

The old man smiled. "Yes, you do."

Madison walked across the room and opened the door. "He wants to see you now. Try not to set fire to the place, will you?"

Spencer scowled. He cautiously stepped inside and eased the door shut behind him.

Bradley motioned with one hand. "Come closer, my son. I need you both right up here next to me."

Spencer walked slowly to the bedside and stood next to Madison. They exchanged glances.

"I know you're both wondering what's going on, so I'll get right to it. You see, I wasn't sure about all this, but when Spencer here showed up today, I knew. I knew that there was more going on here than just fate."

"I haven't been entirely truthful with you two about some things. Madison, you remember the stories I told you about your great grandmother. Well, there are some things I left out. You've always known her as Longberry. Truth is I never told you her name before she married a Longberry. It was York. Her name was Elizabeth York."

"Elizabeth York!" said Spencer. "That's the woman in the photo, the woman I've been chasing."

Madison slowly turned to Spencer. "You've been lusting after my great grandmother?"

"I'm not finished," said Bradley. "You see, Spencer's great grandfather, Harrison, was the one who was actually in love with your great grandmother."

"You can't be serious," said Madison. "Don't tell me she loved him."

"Oh, yes indeed," said Bradley. "They loved each other very much. I was very young at the time, but old enough to see how very much in love they were. In fact, as the years went by, I often remembered those days and those two people and how much they truly loved each other. Few people will ever know that kind of relationship and, fewer still, will understand how it happens."

Spencer was in shock. He said nothing while the old man talked.

"I know this is going to sound pretty strange after what you just told us, but I was with my great grandfather just yesterday."

"That can't be!" shouted Bradley. "Are we talking about Harrison Ellington?"

"That's his name," said Spencer.

Bradley settled back down in his bed. He stared blankly at the ceiling.

"What's the matter, Uncle Bradley?" asked Madison.

"I'm not sure," he said. "My memory is not clear about some of the details, but I always thought your grandfather died a while ago, and here you say he's still alive."

"Well, then, what do you suppose happened to the two of them?" asked Madison.

"I'm not quite sure now."

"Why did you think he had died?" she asked.

"I remember her in mourning and crying for what seemed like forever," said Bradley. "We never saw him again. I just assumed he died."

A long silence fell on the room.

"Uncle Bradley, what was my great grandmother like?" asked Madison.

"She was a lot like you," said Bradley. "She was beautiful, witty, and had a sense of humor like nobody I ever met, which is the real reason I wanted to talk to you both. Do you remember when I said I haven't been entirely truthful? I mentioned once a while back that I always thought there was more jewelry besides the ring. Well, there was a complete set of matching jewelry worth more than you can imagine. Where she got it, I'll never know."

"What became of the jewelry?" asked Madison.

"Like I said before, she had a strange sense of humor. She hid the stuff, and may I say she did a great job. Then she laid out a path of clues to find it. The woman was priceless."

"Clues?" said Spencer. "What kind of clues?"

"That's where the two of you come in. She told me everything, but I was sworn to secrecy. I was told not to tell the whereabouts of the jewelry or how to find it. I was given the ring, but she felt that any descendants should have to work for the remainder of the collection. There are several riddles, I can't remember exactly how many. I do remember her saying that it would take two special people to solve them."

"She made up these riddles decades before we were even born," said Spencer. "How could she have known?"

"There are many things about that woman that will always remain a mystery," said Bradley.

"Still seems odd that she passed up two generations to get to us," said Madison.

"Well, consider this," said Bradley, "she passed it on to me just before she died, and told me to wait."

"Wait for what?" asked Madison.

"That's what I asked her," he replied. "She always was a strange one. She said that I would know when the time was right. Well, look at me. I'm on my last leg lying here in a hospital, and the descendants of both Harrison and her walk in the door to see me. Call me crazy, but it all seems right with me."

Madison gave a quick glance at Spencer. "I know I'm going to regret this, but how do we get started?"

"I'm glad you asked that," said Bradley. "You see, I've known the first clue all these years and quite frankly did not want the responsibility. I mean after all, I'm not even a blood relative. First, I wanted to give it to her son, but I knew he wasn't the right one. Then, I thought it must be his son, but he wasn't fit to give the time of day. Wasn't even sure you were the one, Madison, until now. Good thing too, 'cause I'm running out of time."

"Not to be pushy, Bradley, but we've really piqued our curiosity," said Spencer.

Madison turned to Spencer. "What do you mean by our curiosity? How can you speak for me? You just met me and, with any luck, it will be a short acquaintance."

Spencer stepped back. "When I said that, I didn't mean..."

Bradley smiled. "I told you she's a handful."

"This isn't fair, Uncle Bradley," said Madison. "I'd rather be matched up with Adolph Hitler."

"Sorry, my dear," he said. "But if your great grandmother could see this, she would find it a perfect match."

"Then let's get on with it," she said. "The sooner we find the jewelry, the sooner I can rid myself of what's-his-name."

"Spencer...Spencer Ellington."

"Whatever."

"Spencer, while you're staying in our town, why don't you move into my house," said Bradley. "There's plenty of room."

"Oh no, you don't," said Madison. "I'm staying there, and I'm sure you don't want some stranger in the same house with me."

"He's not a stranger, my dear. In fact, he's practically family."

Madison gave a quick glance at Spencer. "It almost seems illegal or immoral at the very least."

"If it will make you feel any better, he can stay in the room at the other side of the house," said Bradley.

Both Madison and Bradley turned to Spencer as if expecting a comment.

Spencer held out his hands. "Hey, I'm housebroken," he said. "Well, at least, I'm paper-trained."

Bradley cleared his throat. "The one and only clue I can give you goes something like this, "The iron of thunder hides the clue down under."

Spencer leaned over Bradley's bed. "The iron of thunder hides the clue…"

Madison blew a kiss and waved at Bradley. "Got to go, Uncle Bradley. I'll be back again when numb nuts isn't here." She turned and walked out the door.

Spencer quickly said his good-byes and followed her into the hallway. Madison pushed the down button on the elevator.

"So, what's next?" asked Spencer.

"What's next? You're going back to Detroit or wherever you came from. That's what's next."

"I don't think you were listening in there," said Spencer. "Your uncle just put us in charge of finding the jewelry, and that involves the two of us working together."

"Mr. Ellington, I just received a lucrative settlement from my divorce from one of the richest men in America, and I own my own business that has assets in the millions. Why would I want to go on some wild goose chase with you?"

"I really don't know how you could not want to," said Spencer. "This was a wish of your great grandmother. She obviously had you in mind when she hid the jewelry. She's handing you her legacy. It's just not on a silver platter."

The doors of the elevator opened, and Madison stepped inside with Spencer following behind.

"Where do you think you're going?" she asked.

"To the ground floor."

"Then where?"

"To get my things and move into your uncle's house."

"No, you're not."

"Yes, I am," said Spencer, "your uncle invited me."

"My uncle is delirious. He's not in his right mind."

"Seemed okay to me."

"How would you know? You just met him."

Spencer stepped closer. "Hey, look. I'm sorry for that car thingy, but I really think we should get along if we're going to do this thing."

"As in find the jewelry thing," said Madison.

"Precisely."

"By the way, what's in it for you?" she asked. "What do you plan to do with the jewelry when we find it?"

"Sell it and become another one of the richest men in America, you know."

"Oh no you don't. If I were to agree to this Easter egg hunt, and I'm sure I won't, if found, the jewelry would be placed in a safe deposit box where scum and riff-raff like yourself couldn't get at it."

The doors opened, and she started for the front door of the hospital.

"Riff-raff? That's kind of cold, don't you think?" said Spencer.

She opened the door and stopped in front of the hospital. "Do you even have a job?"

"Well, right now, I'm kinda…"

Madison started for the parking lot. "Just like I thought."

Spencer followed behind her. "Okay, so I suppose you're going home to fix us dinner while I go get my stuff."

She stopped beside a Corvette. "Don't bother," she said getting in the car. "I won't let you in the house."

"Okay, if it will make you feel any better, we won't sleep in the same bed," said Spencer.

She slammed the door and started the engine.

"Don't bother fixing anything special," said Spencer as she drove away.

It was late afternoon when Spencer pulled into the driveway. A red Corvette was already there. He got out of his rusted Escort and walked to the front door. There were no lights on and the place looked deserted. He knocked on the door. No answer. He knocked again, still no answer.

"Madison, I know you're in there," he shouted. "Open up."

He peeked in the window, but saw no movement. "Come on, Madison. I don't think this is what your uncle had in mind." He paused. "I'll tell on you if you don't let me in."

It was nearly fifteen minutes later that Spencer climbed into his car and backed out of the driveway. He drove two blocks down the road and parked his car so that he could watch the front of the house.

Nearly two hours passed before the red Corvette backed out of the drive. Spencer started his engine and moved slowly down the street following closely behind her. She turned down side roads and alleys weaving in and out of traffic almost as if she was trying to lose him. She was nearly downtown when she pulled into a parking lot and stopped at the far end. She got out of her car and walked down a brick-lined alley to a restaurant called THE RENDEZ-VOUS.

Spencer parked his car just inside the lot and turned off his engine. He waited until he was sure she had already been seated, got out of his car, and followed her inside the restaurant. It was a rustic, nearly colonial-looking inn with worn tables and dim lighting. He slipped past the standing patrons and walked to the bar at one end of the building. Spencer ordered a beer and searched the room for a woman sitting by herself at a table or booth. He paid for his drink and walked slowly through the dining area casually inspecting each table.

Near the rear of the room Spencer turned the corner and there, sitting in a dark booth, was a tall brunette sipping a drink.

"Good evening," said Spencer, standing next to her table.

"You followed me here, didn't you?" she asked.

"Well, I kinda…"

"You know, even a cretin like you should be able to tell that I don't like you. Besides, I like eating alone which means people like you aren't welcome."

"I know we got off to a bad start, but all I want is fifteen minutes of your time. That's all, and I promise not to bother you again."

Madison paused. "Why am I having trouble believing you?"

Spencer pulled two pieces of paper from his shirt pocket, unfolded them and dropped them on the table.

Madison leaned over the pictures for a moment and then straightened back up. "Uncle Bradley has already showed me the Titanic photo of my great grandmother. You're going to have to do better than that."

Spencer slid the second photo in front of her. "Bet he didn't show you this one."

She glanced at the picture. "What's so special about this one? It's identical to the other one."

"Take a closer look," he said pointing at the picture. "Notice she's holding up her hand in this one, and she's not in this one."

"So, what? Two different photographs."

"That's just it. We enlarged the clock that you see on the deck in the background on both pictures and even the second hand is exactly the same in both."

"Well, then it must be trick photography."

"No such technology in those days."

"Then how do you explain it?" Madison asked.

Spencer smiled. "I think your great grandmother is trying to tell me something."

"You think that a woman who died decades ago is trying to talk to you?"

"Well, something like that," muttered Spencer.

Madison slowly shook her head. "See, that's the kind of thing that confirms my suspicions that you're one sandwich short of a picnic. Now I'm going to have to ask you to leave or I'm calling the manager."

"I swear to you I'm not crazy," said Spencer. "Although there have been times when this whole thing has seemed like a nightmare, what with the messages and the dreams."

Madison froze. "What dreams?"

"The dreams about Elizabeth York."

"What happens in those dreams?"

"Different things."

"Is there someone chasing her down the halls of a sinking ship?" asked Madison.

"Yeah," said Spencer, taking a seat across from Madison. "You've had the same dreams, haven't you?"

"That doesn't necessarily make us buddies, you know."

"It's almost as if your great grandmother, Elizabeth York, has been trying to unite you and me," said Spencer. "Why, I don't know. I got the impression that I was supposed to warn you about something."

"Maybe you were supposed to warn me about an impending car fire," said Madison.

Spencer gave her a quick glance, then smiled. "Maybe so I wouldn't forget the marshmallows."

Madison fought to hold back the laughter. "All of my instincts tell me to run, not walk, away from you."

"Does this mean I can stay at your uncle's house?"

"Don't push it."

Spencer gulped his beer. "I know you don't want to hear this, but I fell in love with you the minute I saw that photo of your great grandmother."

"Let's get one thing straight," said Madison. "You fell in love with Elizabeth York, not Madison Riley."

"I know you'll think I'm crazy, but I think she was leading me to you."

"I think you're crazy, but for a lot more reasons than that," she said.

Spencer positioned the two pictures in front of her. "These are identical photographs, and yet in this one, she is holding up her hand. At first, we thought she was pointing at the pendant around her neck. Then we realized she was trying to show us the ring. The ring on her finger is the same one that was stolen from your uncle and the same one that is in all the news right now."

"Why would she want us to go after the ring?" asked Madison. "It belongs to someone else."

"It's not the ring that she's concerned about," said Spencer. "It's the rest of the collection. I think that's what she wants you and me to go after."

Madison shook her head. "It's just too preposterous. Dead people don't send messages to the living."

"How do you know?" asked Spencer. "Nobody knows for sure what dead people can do or can't do. Besides, how do you explain these two photos?"

"Maybe two different cameras took the same picture at exactly the same time."

"If they snapped the pictures at exactly the same second, how do you explain the hand showing in one and not in the other?"

Madison paused. She finished the last bite of her dinner and set her fork on the table. "You got me there," she said and got to her feet. "All I know is that it's been a long day, and I want to go home."

Spencer stood as well. "Does that mean I can come over to stay?"

Madison first stared at Spencer and then turned to look out the window. "You can have a room on the older side of the house."

"I'll be good. I promise," said Spencer. "I need to go to my motel and pick up my things."

She dropped money on the table and started for the door. Once they were outside, she walked across the parking lot towards her car.

"Is that your car parked so close to mine?" she asked.

"Yes, that's mine," said Spencer.

"You parked so close I can't get into my car."

"I'll move mine, so that you can get into yours," said Spencer. He slid between the cars and opened the door. Carefully, he squeezed himself in his car and closed the door behind him. Unfortunately, as he did, he caught the bottom of Madison's skirt in the door. She looked down just as he started the engine.

"Hey!" she shouted and pulled away from the car. As she did, he put the car in gear and lurched forward tearing the skirt from her body.

Spencer brought the car to a stop. He opened the door to get out, and the shredded skirt fell to the ground. He first glanced at it and then turned to Madison. She was standing in the street with only a blouse and panties, her hands covering her crotch.

"Look what you've done!" she shouted.

"Oh, I'm so sorry," said Spencer picking up the torn garment.

"You're an idiot! You know that?"

"It was an accident. I really didn't…"

"No, it wasn't! You did this on purpose, now give me that!"

Spencer walked towards her carrying the skirt. He was within ten feet of her when he stopped. "No, you come and get it," he said. "I've taken just about all the abuse I'm going to take from you."

"Abuse?" said Madison. "You talk to me about abuse? Who set fire to my car? Who bothered me while I'm eating, and who ripped the very clothes from my body? And you have the nerve to accuse me of abusing you!"

"You know, I'm sure your mother taught you please and thank you, so I don't blame her. I figure you lost your manners the same time you came into money," said Spencer. He held out the skirt in front of him. "So as far as I'm concerned, if you want this, you're going to have to give me a please and a thank you, and you're going to have to come over here to get it."

Madison's eyebrows furrowed, her eyes were slits. "You'll pay for this, Spencer whatever-your-name-is."

"Ellington. Spencer Ellington is the name."

She climbed into her car and slammed the door. As she drove off, Spencer tossed the skirt into the open window of the car.

Spencer stopped by the motel to pick up his clothes, and it was nearly an hour later before he pulled into Bradley's driveway. He got out of his car and started for the front door when he noticed the front door was standing open. He cautiously stepped inside. Chairs were upset and shredded.

Paintings were broken and laying on the floor. He stared at the mess that stretched across the living room and beyond.

Madison walked into the room. "The place is ransacked!" she said. "I think we've been robbed!"

 # Chapter Thirteen

It was nearly 8:30 when Charlie Stenger opened the door to his office. Jim Hastings was already at his desk.

"You sure picked a morning to be late," said Jim. "The boss wants to see you in his office."

"Oh, Christ! What does that asshole want?"

"I don't know, but he seemed upset," said Jim. "I wouldn't keep him waiting either because he knows you've been late three times this week alone."

Charlie scowled at Jim. "And I wonder how he found that out."

"Hey, don't look at me. God knows I've had my share of mornings when I'm a little late."

"Yeah, but I'll bet you don't point that out to Gibbs." He turned and started for the door. "I'd better go see what shithead wants."

The door was open to Mr. Gibb's office, and Charlie stepped inside. Mr. Gibbs was sitting at his desk.

"You wanted to see me, Mr. Gibbs?" asked Charlie.

"Well, Charlie, my boy," said Mr. Gibbs. "If you don't mind, close that door behind you and take a seat." He cleared his throat. "Something has come to my attention, and I think we need to talk about it."

Charlie slowly closed the door and sat in one of the two high-back chairs across from Mr. Gibbs. "I suppose you're a little upset with my attendance lately. I want you to know that I just bought a new alarm clock, and that should…"

"Charlie, I understand you have been spending company time researching the claim that was made following the Titanic disaster."

Charlie sat up in his chair. "Well, I did look up a few…"

"You see, that's the kind of thing that goes on around here that we just can't put up with," said Mr. Gibbs.

"Mr. Gibbs, I wasn't doing this for personal gain," said Charlie. "I don't think the jewelry went down on the Titanic. I think it's somewhere here in America."

"You know lying about this won't help matters any," said Mr. Gibbs pausing for effect. "I'm afraid I'm going to have to make an example out of you for the others. We're going to have to let you go, Charlie old man. I'm sure you understand."

"Let me go? You can't do this! I have twenty years in the company."

"We can, and we did."

Charlie's jaw tightened. "It was that goddamn Hastings down there who ratted on me, wasn't it?"

"I don't think at this point that it matters who was the informer, the important thing is that we correct this problem."

"I'll get that weasel, one way or the other," muttered Charlie.

"You're free to go, Mr. Stenger. We will send you your personal belongings and your last check. Good luck to you."

Charlie got to his feet and started for the door. "You know, I was only going for the reward," said Charlie. "I was going to turn the jewelry in and ask for a reward, but the important point here is that Mutual would recover millions of dollars' worth of jewelry, money they paid out years ago."

"As well you should, Mr. Stenger."

"However, after today my plans have changed," said Charlie, opening the door. "Now, when I find the jewelry, and I will find it, I'm not sharing it with anybody, especially you."

"Now, just a minute, Mr. Stenger, you can't..."

"And tell that creep, Hastings that I'm going to get him for this," said Charlie and slammed the door behind him.

It was a long trip back home for Charlie. He muttered aloud most of the way about how he was going to get that Hastings guy and how he would find the jewelry and become the richest man in America. When interviewed on the six o'clock news, he would make a point of holding the jewelry up to the camera and send a special message to Gibbs and The Mutual Insurance Company.

He stopped in front of his apartment and got out of his car. Two men were pacing in front of his door. As he got closer, Charlie could see it was the Luigi brothers.

"I called your work, and they said you got canned," said Frank. "What happened?"

Charlie unlocked the front door and walked inside. "Some guy ratted on me and got me fired," said Charlie. "I might need you two to do a small favor for me later on."

Frank and his brother followed behind.

"They say you can only get fired for two things, screwing the help or stealing," said Frank. "Since you're uglier than I am and I'm sure no woman would have you, what did you steal?"

"Very funny," said Charlie. "What are you two idiots doing here anyway?"

"Idiots?" said Frank. "You're calling my brother and me idiots? I'll have you know in high school I scored high enough on the SAT test to go to college."

"Did you go?" asked Charlie.

"Go where?"

"To college!"

Frank cleared his throat and looked away. "I gave it a try."

"Flunked out, didn't you?"

"I may have had a few problems adjusting to…"

Charlie smiled. "You're too stupid for college. It's as simple as that."

Frank pondered the point and decided to change the subject. "We paid a visit to your friend, Madison Riley, and came up with nothing."

"Did you rough her up a bit?"

"She wasn't even there."

"Well, what did you do?"

"We searched for the jewelry, like you told us."

"I told you to get her to tell you," said Charlie. "You two couldn't count your testicles twice and come up with the same answer."

"Well, I don't think the jewelry is in that house," said Frank. "We pretty much tore the guts out of that place."

Charlie leaned forward. "Listen, you guys, the gloves are off. I don't care what you have to do to find that jewelry. I'm dedicating my whole life to finding it. I've got old scores to settle, and besides that it's worth a shit load of money. We'll never have to work again in our lives."

"Sounds good to me, Charlie," said Frank. "If she knows where it is, we'll get it from her. You can count on us."

Charlie stood and thrust out his hand. "Now, go get some answers."

Frank shook his hand. "It's as good as done."

 # CHAPTER FOURTEEN

It took Madison and Spencer nearly an hour to clean and straighten the house. They both collapsed into chairs and leaned back to rest. Spencer glanced at a pile of tapestries on the floor.

"Where did all the rugs come from?" asked Spencer.

"They're not rugs," said Madison. "They're tapestries, expensive tapestries from the Middle East. My uncle had them hanging across that wall. The hoodlums who broke in must have torn them down."

"Makes more sense to have them on the floor. You can't wipe your feet on them when they're up there."

"Good Lord, man! Are you always this crude?" she said. "Don't you have any sense of style?"

"Hey, lady, in my circles, people put their rugs on the floor at the back door," said Spencer.

"It's fashionable to hang expensive tapestries on the wall, not that you would know anything about fashion."

"Why do you suppose they took them down?"

"Who knows?" she said. "Probably just to be mean."

"I think they were trying to find something like a safe in the wall."

"That's absurd," said Madison. "I've been in and out of this house all my life, and I never heard anything about a safe."

"I'm sure you have," said Spencer. "But don't forget, the jewelry would have been hidden long before you were born. A lot can happen to a house over the years."

Silence followed. Madison spotted the luggage by the front door.

"I can't believe I'm allowing you to stay here after that stunt you pulled at the restaurant," she said.

"That wasn't a stunt," said Spencer, sitting up in his chair. "That was an accident."

"There's no way that was an accident. You did that on purpose."

"Actually, it was your fault. You were standing too close to the car. You deserved what you got."

"My fault? You slam a car door on my skirt, rip it from my body, and it's my fault? Spoken like a true man."

"Well, there's that female logic for you," said Spencer. "You stand so close to a car that you get your skirt caught in it, and it's my fault. Incredible!"

"You did it to see me naked, didn't you?"

"What?"

"You're no different than any other man. You'll do anything to see a beautiful woman without her clothes on."

"Oh, aren't we a little caught up with ourselves?"

"Well, it's true. All men are pigs," said Madison.

Spencer bristled. He moved to the edge of his seat. "In the first place, I didn't do it on purpose, and in the second place, you're not that hot with your skirt off."

"Not that hot? Is that what you said? I was hot enough for you to look, you pervert!"

"Pervert! Who are you calling a pervert?"

"All men are perverts," said Madison, "and you're no exception."

"Okay, now let me get this straight," said Spencer. "You wear a low, plunging neckline that exposes your breasts, and if a man actually looks at the exposed flesh, he's a pervert. Is that about right?"

"That's exactly what I'm talking about."

"Then why do you wear them?"

"Why do we wear what?"

"The plunging neckline. Why do you wear clothes that expose a part of your body that everyone knows excites a man sexually?"

"We wear clothes that accentuate our bodies. It makes us feel pretty."

Spencer laughed. "You don't believe that crap, do you? It's all a part of the natural order of things. Females have been luring males into their traps since the beginning of time. I wouldn't doubt Eve wore a short skirt when she brought that apple to Adam."

"I should have known," said Madison.

"What?"

"You're a chauvinist as well," she said. "It figures though. Someone with your basic, primal needs and goals in life would consider women to be less than an equal."

Spencer ran his fingers through his hair in frustration. He scanned the room, his eyes stopping on a portrait of Elizabeth York hanging on the wall. It was a large portrait nearly six feet in height and four feet wide. The frame was bold and masterfully sculpted to match the painting. Elizabeth was posed standing with her back against the wall and her head turned.

"I fell in love with that woman over there," he said, pointing at the work of art. "I'll bet she wasn't as mouthy as her great granddaughter."

"Uncle Bradley said I am a carbon copy of her," said Madison. "Besides, who are you calling mouthy?"

Spencer slowly shook his head and got to his feet. "You know, we're both tired and you're grouchy. Why don't you show me to my room, and we'll get some sleep?"

Madison stood and started across the room. "I can't believe I'm letting someone as rude as you sleep in the same house with me."

Spencer grabbed his bags and followed. "Don't forget, Uncle Bradley always liked me best."

"The bedrooms are all upstairs. You're sleeping in a room over here at the back of the house." She opened the door and Spencer stepped inside. It was small, about the size of a broom closet with a wooden floor and no windows.

"You can't expect me to sleep in here! There isn't a bed!" said Spencer.

"Uncle Bradley said you could stay in his house, but I'm telling you where you will sleep."

"Come on, lady," said Spencer. "There must be four to five beds upstairs. I promise I will not leave my room."

"Six bedrooms, and not one with your name on it," she said and walked away. "Have a good night."

+++

It was nearly six o'clock in the morning when Madison swung open the door to the storage room. Spencer was curled in a fetal position lying on the floor. He was wearing his pants but had fashioned a pillow by rolling up his shirt. The light from the kitchen streaked across the room and fell onto Spencer. He winced and slowly stretched his legs.

"My God, what time is it?" he muttered.

"Six o'clock," said Madison. "I let you sleep in."

Spencer slowly sat up. "Six o'clock! It's still nighttime. The day doesn't begin until noon. That's the way God planned it. We get up at noon and twelve hours later at midnight we go to bed."

"Why does that not surprise me?" said Madison. She turned and walked across the kitchen.

Spencer rolled over on his knees. "Dear God, that floor is as hard as her heart." He slowly rose to his feet flexing his legs and arms. "And what did you mean by that crack about not surprising you?"

Madison put a skillet on the stove and turned on the heat. She opened the refrigerator and took out the eggs.

"You have no ambition, no drive. You don't even have a job. Instead of finding a job, you chase after a woman who has been dead for years. If you don't mind my saying so, your type doesn't have the self-discipline to get up in the morning. Quite frankly, you're lazy."

Spencer trudged across the kitchen and sat down at the table. "Hey, don't sugar coat it, Miss Perfect. Tell it like it is."

Madison cracked two eggs and dropped them in the skillet. "Okay, so tell me. When was the last time you got up to an alarm clock?"

"I don't know whether you know it or not, but Thomas Edison did some of his best work at night," said Spencer. "And I don't think he even owned an alarm clock."

Madison turned and scowled. "That's because he didn't sleep."

The eggs crackled, and the aroma drifted across the room. Spencer lifted his head and sniffed. "No chance you might drop two more of those beauties in that pan?"

She flipped the eggs and turned down the heat on the burner. "I have agreed to allow you to stay in this house only because my uncle insisted, but he didn't say anything about feeding you. Besides, I don't feed anybody who rips my clothes off."

"Might do you some good," muttered Spencer.

"What did you say?"

"I said I think you need to get laid."

"My God, have you always been this rude?"

"I'm just stating the obvious," he said.

She slid the eggs from the skillet onto a plate and took a seat across from Spencer. "Have you noticed how much you irritate me? I've only known you for less than a day, and I already hate you."

Spencer smiled. "You'll change your mind. After all, I've already learned to accept you for who you are."

"Accept me? You've learned to accept me?"

"You're not a very easy person to get along with. You're arrogant, rude, you've got your nose in the air, and anybody who would eat in front of me, I have to learn to accept."

Madison took a bite of her eggs. "You're jealous, aren't you?"

"Of what?"

"Of my money. You're jealous of my money."

"It all comes back to money with you, doesn't it?" said Spencer. "Nothing in your life is more important."

"Spoken like a true loser. You hate it because I'm a woman and worth millions."

"Christ, lady! Everyone knows where you got your money! It's from the man in your life, not the woman that you are."

"I started my own business and built it to the success that it is all by myself. I had no help from any man."

"Where did you get the money to start the business?"

Madison set down her fork. "Huh?"

"You heard me. Where did you get the money to start the business?"

"My husband may have loaned me a few dollars in the beginning."

Spencer grinned. "Just as I thought."

"That's not the point," she said. "I still successfully developed the business."

"No, that is the point," said Spencer. "Most Americans would love to have their own business, but can't afford to get it started. They simply don't have a sugar daddy like you did."

A silence fell on the room. Madison finished her eggs and wiped her mouth with a napkin. "You know the sooner we find that jewelry, the sooner we part company. I have business to attend to at the office, so what do you need to help you find the treasure?"

"I need the family photos," said Spencer.

Madison got up to leave. "We have albums of them. I'll stack them on the dining room table. Anything else?"

Spencer paused. "No, nothing I can think of."

"Good, then let's get this thing over with as soon as possible," said Madison, starting for the door. "The less I see of you the better I'll like it."

+++

It was after nine o'clock, and nightfall had settled on the streets of Memphis. Madison had research to do and had stopped by the library on her way home from the office. She picked out an armful of books and found a comfortable armchair. Within minutes, she leaned her head back and closed her eyes.

A hand lightly tapped her on the shoulder. "Ma'am," said a young man leaning over her, "the library is closing."

Madison jumped and opened her eyes. "Huh? What?"

"I'm sorry, ma'am, but the library is closing," he said stepping back.

She glanced around the room. The room was empty. She turned to the young man standing next to her. "In other words, get out of here so you can go home."

He smiled. "Something like that," he said.

She picked up the books in front of her, hesitated, then set them back down. She was tired and just wanted to go home. She picked up her purse and started for the door.

It was a warm evening and the cool breeze from the west felt good as Madison stepped outside. She started down the steps of the library to the sidewalk below. There was nobody in sight. However, Madison thought it strange there was nobody in sight, on the streets, sidewalks, or in cars. She paused, as she looked both ways down the street. She turned and found the library was dark now. Madison had an eerie feeling she could not explain. Maybe it was because her head was still foggy from having just woken up.

She started across the street to her car that was parked on the other side. As she got closer, she dug in her purse for her car keys. She pointed the remote access button at the car and unlocked the doors. As she grabbed the handle, out of the corner of her eye, she noticed headlights coming on. She turned in their direction. Someone in a parked car had started the engine and turned on the headlights. She stared at the vehicle, it did not move. She felt a chill. Something was happening she could not explain. She felt threatened and decided to make her escape.

She opened the car and slid into the driver's seat. As she started the engine, she glanced in the rearview mirror. The headlights were moving. The car was slowly moving into the street. Madison pulled away from the curb and started down the street. At the first intersection, she turned left. The car behind followed her around the corner. She sped up, and the car behind kept pace.

Madison knew evasive action was useless, the driver was obviously more skilled than she was. She decided to race home as fast as she could and hope that Spencer would be there to help. She punched the accelerator. It was only a few blocks, and she knew that if she gained a lead it would give her more time when she reached the house.

She pulled into her driveway and drove across the lawn to her front door. She scrambled out of the car and ran to the porch. She heard the screeching of tires as a vehicle came to a stop in the street. Spencer heard the commotion and opened the door. Madison fell into his arms.

"Spencer! Thank God you're here!" she said, still holding him.

"It's a dream come true," said Spencer folding his arms around her.

"A car followed me home from the library," she said turning to the street.

Spencer let her go and stepped outside. A car turned off its headlights and sped away.

"Why did they turn off their lights?" asked Madison.

"So that we couldn't see the license tag," said Spencer. "Are you okay?"

"Yes, I'm fine."

"Any idea who it was?"

"I have no idea," she replied. "They were waiting for me to leave the library though, of that I'm certain."

Spencer led her to the sofa, and they both sat down. "This confirms what I've been thinking. I think the break in and vandalism was not just a kid's prank. I think someone is looking for the jewelry."

"Why do you say that?" asked Madison.

"What they did in this house was not just an act of maliciousness, they were searching for something. If they had been kids vandalizing your house, there would have been more things broken. As it was, hardly anything was destroyed. Now someone is following you. It all fits."

"How did they find out about the jewelry?"

"I don't know," said Spencer. "Maybe they saw the story on TV."

"I still think we should go to the police."

"Not just yet," said Spencer. "I promise we will if they start playing rough. I just don't want the police involved until we find the jewelry."

Madison took a deep breath. "Thanks," she said with a warm smile.

"Thanks for what?" asked Spencer.

"I don't know...just for being here."

"You're welcome, I'm sure."

Spencer stretched and got to his feet. "Guess I should turn in now. Didn't sleep too good on that floor."

"I was thinking about that," she said. "Seems a waste having all those bedrooms upstairs and you're having to sleep on the floor. Tell you what, you can have the room at the end of the hall. It's haunted anyway."

"Haunted?"

"You're going to like this part," said Madison. "That's the room your Elizabeth York stayed in."

Spencer glanced at the ceiling. "Well, isn't that interesting?"

"I'm sure that's one ghost you wouldn't mind seeing."

"Why the sudden change of heart?" asked Spencer. "I thought I was forever doomed to the storage room."

Madison smiled. "I don't know, you don't appear to be some kind of a murderer, rapist, or such. Besides, I got to thinking how romantic that you would fall in love with a woman who lived so long ago. You must be a sensitive and caring man."

"My ex-wife doesn't think so."

"They say you get out of a relationship what you put into it," said Madison. "Maybe she wasn't trying hard enough."

Spencer smiled. "How 'bout you? Were you trying hard enough in your marriage?"

"Obviously not," she said.

They stared into each other's eyes for a moment, then Madison said, "Well, let's get some sleep. Tomorrow is another day."

Spencer grabbed his things and they both climbed the stairs. At the top of the stairs, Spencer looked down a long, dark hallway that connected six bedrooms and a communal bathroom. They stopped in front of her room.

Madison pointed down the hall. "That's the bathroom, third door down on the right." She paused. "Do you shower in the mornings?"

"Didn't used to, but I'm turning over a new leaf. Six o'clock in the morning is my new time for starting my day."

"I'll let you go first. Gives me a few more minutes of sleep."

She turned and opened the door halfway. "Well, good night," she said, still standing in the open doorway.

Spencer froze. He didn't know whether to lightly kiss her, shake her hand, or simply say good night and walk away. It had been such a rocky relationship from the beginning, and yet she seemed to have softened. He wasn't quite sure why. The incident with the car following her seemed to frighten her, but hardly enough for her to forget the fact that he had destroyed her car and ripped her skirt off with his car door.

"It's too soon," she blurted to help him decide. "Good night," she said and closed the door behind her.

With a sense of both relief and disappointment, Spencer continued on down the hallway to the last door. Slowly, he opened the door and stepped inside. It was just as he thought it would be, with bold, flowery wallpaper framed in rich, dark mahogany woodwork. An ornate canopy bed stood in the middle of the room with dark walnut furniture throughout.

Spencer dropped his luggage and sat on the edge of the bed. It was a room that had belonged to a woman. There was no doubt of that. It had a feminine air about it and yet boldly feminine, strong-willed with a touch of wit and humor. This was a woman decisive in nature, determined in will, and yet unafraid to relax her femininity if necessary.

Spencer gazed around the room at the portraits that hung on the walls. Richly detailed and well preserved, the works of art gave the room an almost regal look. In front of a window was a small table that held a collection of old framed photographs. Spencer walked across the room and leaned over the table. His eyes fell on the one in the center of the collection. It was of Elizabeth. She was walking arm-in-arm with a man dressed in a suit and a hat stylishly tipped over one eye. He strained to see if he could identify the man, but with the shadow created by the hat and the bushy moustache, his facial features were hidden from view. He suspected the man was his own great grandfather, but there was no way of being sure.

Next to that picture was a slightly smaller framed photo of a young boy sitting at a table in front of a birthday cake. A neatly stacked pile of presents was sitting next to him, while other boys and girls surrounded the table and looked on. Spencer wondered if the birthday boy was Uncle Bradley. He would try to remember to ask Madison tomorrow.

Spencer got undressed and walked across the room to snap off the overhead light. Just before flipping the switch, he glanced around the room. It felt good to be in this room that belonged to Elizabeth York. He turned off the light and got into bed. Spencer smiled to himself. It had been a good day. He rolled over and fell fast asleep.

 # CHAPTER FIFTEEN

Madison woke to the sound of running water. She turned and looked at the clock. It was six o'clock just as he said. If nothing else, he was true to his word. He said he would shower at six, and that he did. She rolled out of bed and slipped on her robe. It was time to fix breakfast, and maybe she might crack an extra two eggs for her guest.

Madison stepped into the hallway. She could hear the shower running and Spencer humming some childhood song, the name of which she could not remember. As she turned to the stairway, she heard the water shut off, and Spencer cry out, "Oh, shit! Madison, are you out there?"

She hurried down the hall and opened the bathroom door. Spencer was still in the shower, his head peeking out.

"What's wrong?" she asked.

"I forgot a towel," said Spencer. "Can you get me one?"

"You mean you walked down here with nothing on?"

Spencer pointed across the room at a robe hanging on the back of a door. "I wore that. Hope you don't mind."

"That's a woman's robe. Did it fit?"

"Barely, now could you please get me a towel? It's getting cold in here."

Madison returned to the hallway and opened a linen closet. She grabbed the smallest towel she could find and returned to the bathroom. This time she barged through the door and stood in the center of the room.

"Hey, what are you doing? I'm naked here."

Madison smiled. "You wanted a towel and I got you one."

"I appreciate it, now you can go."

Her smile grew bolder. "Do you remember the incident where you left me naked in the street?"

"Huh?"

"You completely removed my skirt leaving me standing there in public with only my underwear on. Does any of this ring a bell?"

"It wasn't my fault," said Spencer. "You were standing too close to my car."

"But if I had never met you, if you had never come into my life, this embarrassing moment would never have happened."

"Well, I suppose…"

Madison threw the towel over her shoulder, picked the robe from the hook and threw it over the same shoulder. "You'll find these in your room," she said and walked out the door.

"Oh, come on, Madison," said Spencer. "You can't do that."

"Beats standing in the street in your underwear," she shouted as she walked down the hall.

Spencer burst into the kitchen, his hair still wet, but he was fully dressed. Madison slid two sizzling eggs onto a plate and two more onto another. She added bacon and toast and handed him a plate.

"Sit down and eat while it's still hot," she said.

"Wait a minute," said Spencer. "Just yesterday, I sat here and watched you eat in front of me. Now, I'm sleeping in a bed and you're cooking for me."

"Don't let it go to your head."

Spencer took a seat at the table. "There's only one explanation for this, you kinda like me, don't you?"

Madison sat down across from Spencer. "I told you not to let this go to your head."

"You like me. It's as simple as that. Oh, it might not be the kind of like that moves mountains, but you like me just the same."

"You're pretty sure of yourself, aren't you?"

"Sure enough to know that much," said Spencer. He paused as he took a bite of his breakfast. "Tell me something, what was it like being married to one of the richest men in America?"

"It wasn't what you think," she replied.

"How do you know what I'm thinking?"

"You're thinking that it was all fun and games," said Madison. "It wasn't even that good in the beginning. I don't know why he ever got married, he had no time for a wife, or anybody else for that matter."

"You must have got a lot of nice things," said Spencer.

"On my last birthday, he sent one of his aides to buy me something," said Madison. "The guy even signed the card for him. That's when I knew it was time to get out. I'm not even real sure he knows I'm gone. The man knew how to make money, I'll give him that, but he didn't know the first thing about a woman's heart."

Spencer leaned back in his chair. "Let me guess, your folks were incredibly rich."

"My father was a diplomat of sorts," said Madison. "We lived in eighteen different countries while I was growing up. Rich? I suppose he was. He kept things like that to himself."

"What do you mean a diplomat of sorts? Come to think of it, I'm not sure what a diplomat is."

"When the President needs someone to negotiate with a foreign head-of-state, he would call my dad," said Madison. "He was, as they say, a closer. He got the job done."

"You're talking about the president of General Motors or Ford, aren't you?" asked Spencer.

"My father was one of the few people in the world who had a phone number that got him straight to the President of the United States."

"I'm impressed," said Spencer.

"What was really impressive was to know my father. He was truly an incredible man when it came to negotiations. I swear if they would have let him, he could have talked the Arabs into giving us their oil."

"You speak of your parents in the past tense," said Spencer. "What happened to them?"

"They were killed by insurgents in South America," said Madison. "What they did to my parents is unspeakable, and the sad part is, he was working on behalf of the same people who killed them."

"I'm so sorry," said Spencer.

"He died doing what he loved to do, and mother was by his side, which is where she wanted to be."

"Sounds like they were wonderful people," said Spencer.

Madison said nothing. She paused, forced a smile, and said, "So, how about you? What was your marriage like?"

"You don't want to know," said Spencer.

"Come on. I spilled my guts," said Madison.

"There's an old joke that goes something like this. Why did the bride smile on her way down the aisle? She knew she would never have to have sex again. My ex had the biggest smile you ever saw."

"I take it your wife wasn't into sex," said Madison.

"She considered sex to be a four-letter word."

"Maybe the problem was you. Maybe you were doing it all wrong."

Spencer scowled, "Oh, please."

"Typical macho male," said Madison. "It's always the woman's fault."

"Don't start with me," said Spencer. "You and I have been getting along after a really shaky start."

Madison smiled. "You're right. So, tell me about your parents. What was your father like?"

"That's the difference between you and me," said Spencer. "You had a father, I had a Pop."

"So, what was he like?"

Spencer leaned back. "I was only about eight or nine years old as I recall and thought I was the toughest guy in the world, now that I was the proud owner of a BB gun.

I remember that it was only a couple days after he gave me that gun, that I was in back of the house shooting at just about anything in sight. I didn't know it at the time, but he was watching me from a window when, suddenly, I began shooting at the birds sitting high up in the trees. I don't know whether I actually believed that I could hit one of them. They seemed so far off. Maybe I thought of them as some kind of inanimate object. I don't know. All I know is that it wasn't long before I scored a direct hit, and to my surprise, a bird began its descent from its perch, falling gracelessly as it bounced from one limb to another. I must say I was surprised. I never really thought that I would shoot one."

"I remember that I walked over to the bird with a certain amount of apprehension. I wasn't sure if I should strut like some big game hunter after the kill, or cautiously creep up to the innocent little animal that I had needlessly destroyed. I knelt beside the fallen bird, and with the end of my gun, I gently turned it over. From its pale red underside, I knew that it was a female robin. I remember wishing that it was only stunned, and that it would suddenly awaken and fly away, but that was not to be. Her head dangled, lifelessly, to one side, and a small trickle of blood oozed from under her feathers and dripped onto the ground."

I nudged the bird with my gun hoping to arouse it from some deep sleep. Nothing. By now, the tears were flowing from my eyes as I finally came to realize what I had done. A sweet and innocent life had been taken, and it was my fault."

"I don't know how long he had been standing beside me, but suddenly, he was there bending down on one knee. He stayed there for the longest time. I remember that. I was dying inside. I felt so bad. I had done something very bad and deserved to be punished, and he calmly stared at the dead bird."

"Finally, he turned to me and asked me if I understood what had happened here. I muttered something about an accident and how I'd never do it again and then he told me something that I never forgot. In fact, I'm sure that was his intention that it would be a day that I would remember all my life. He told me that today was the day that the life of a small bird ended. Hardly seems significant in the big scheme of things, but nonetheless, we have one less bird in the world today. Tomorrow, there will be one less song being sung by a creature whose only goal in life is to give happiness."

"He then laid a hand on my shoulder, and when I finally worked up the nerve to look him in the eye, I noticed a tear falling down his cheek. To this day, I can't remember another time that I ever saw him cry. He told me that since God loves all life, even the lowly robin, and there must be a reason for this seemingly senseless death. It was then that he told me something that would guide my life from then on. He told me that, without doubt, God sacrificed that little bird so that I would learn a valuable lesson. I would be a better person after having seen how precious life is. Life must be preserved at all costs. Then, he told me that I should always remember the lesson that I learned so that the robin's dying would not be in vain."

"What a wonderful story," said Madison. "I didn't know sensitive men like that existed."

"I spent yesterday going through your family photo album," said Spencer. "I must say from the pictures I saw, you had a beautiful mother and a very handsome father."

"My mother won several beauty contests in her day, even after she was a grown adult."

"I can see why," said Spencer. "I saw many pictures of you as a teenager. You were a very pretty girl."

"I was a very pretty girl?"

Spencer paused, then smiled. "You got me," he said. "You'd think I'd learn."

"Just teasing you."

"I could see that you liked to ride," said Spencer. "Must have been a million photos of you on horses."

"That was one horse you saw in those photos," said Madison. "The greatest horse that ever lived."

"I take it this horse belonged to you."

"For ten years, until he died a while back," said Madison as she stared out the window. "His name was Thunder. God, how I miss that animal." Her voice cracked as she spoke, and her eyes welled with tears.

Spencer changed the conversation. "So, your Uncle Bradley is the last survivor of the Titanic. You must be proud."

Madison wiped her eyes and forced a smile. "Oh, I'm proud of him. That's for sure, but not because he is the last survivor, rather because of the man he became."

"Wish he'd tell us where the jewelry is," said Spencer.

"That would be cheating," said Madison. "Besides, he promised he wouldn't tell us."

"Speaking of the jewelry, let's get started with the first clue."

"I don't even remember what it was," said Madison.

"I wrote it down," said Spencer. He reached in his pocket and pulled out a slip of paper. "The iron of thunder hides the clues down under. Now, I've been thinking about this clue. I noticed on the roof of this house there is a lightning rod. I'm thinking that's the iron of thunder."

Madison scowled. "What does a lightning rod have to do with the iron of thunder?"

"Lightning rods are made out of some kind of metal, which I suppose could be iron, and thunder represents storms and lightening. It might be a bit of a stretch."

Madison's face turned sour. "A bit of a stretch?" she said. "That's about the most incredible leap I ever heard."

"Oh, and I suppose you could do better?"

"Couldn't do any worse."

"Okay, let's hear your idea," said Spencer. "You're such a hot shot. Come on. I want to hear your idea."

Madison slowly shook her head and smiled. "What are we doing here? We need to work together on this instead of fighting all the time."

Spencer paused. "Well, maybe the lightening rod thing was a little far-fetched. Let's take another look at it. We know there's only one kind of thunder, but many things made of iron, so let's concentrate on the iron."

The room grew silent. Spencer got up and poured a cup of coffee.

Madison jumped. "That's it!"

"What's it?"

"You're wrong about there only being one kind of thunder. My horse was called Thunder."

"You're right, and that makes sense," said Spencer. "And the iron would be his horseshoe."

"Okay, so how does it go again? The iron of thunder..."

"The iron of thunder hides the clue down under."

"What does it mean down under?"

Spencer thought for a moment. "It must mean the clue is hidden under the ground where Thunder walked."

"The only ground I can think of is the track where Thunder raced, but that won't work. We can't dig up the whole track."

"What about a stable?" asked Spencer. "Where did you keep Thunder?"

"The Diluciano Stables just outside of town."

Spencer got to his feet. "Let's go."

# Chapter Sixteen

The fresh country air felt good to Spencer. Even though he was born and bred in the city, he always had a sense of yearning for the farmlands of rural America. Following Madison's directions, he turned down an unpaved lane that was lined with a white board fence. The lane took them to the back of the house where he parked near the barn.

"This is it," said Madison, slowly getting out of the car. It was a large, white farmhouse with clothes hanging on the line. There was a barn, silo, and outbuildings all painted white.

Spencer got out of the car and surveyed the area. "Funny, I don't see any horses," he said.

"The pastures are all grown over with weeds," said Madison.

They walked to the back porch and knocked on the door. After a brief moment, the door opened, and an older woman with gray hair and tired eyes stood looking out.

"Betty Diluciano?" said Madison.

The old woman studied Madison for a moment. "Madison, is that you?" The two women embraced. "I haven't seen you since you were just a girl."

Madison turned to Spencer. "I want you to meet Spencer…"

"Spencer Ellington," he said offering his hand.

"Pleased to meet you," she said, taking his hand. "So, what brings you out to this ghost town?"

"Business a little slow?" asked Madison.

"Only got two boarders anymore," said Betty. "Remember a time when the farm was full of horses. Had more than we could take care of. Things will pick up though. I'm sure of it."

"Would you mind if we took a look at Thunder's stable?" asked Madison.

"My goodness, help yourself. Retired that stable after Thunder died, you know. Never was and never will be a horse to match the likes of that animal. What are you looking for?"

"Just wanted to look around for old time sakes if you don't mind."

"Go right on ahead. You won't be bothering anything, that's for sure."

"Nice seeing you again," said Madison.

"Take care, child," said Betty.

Madison stopped at the doorway of the barn and studied the structure. Small piles of peeled paint lay in the weeds surrounding the building. Windows were broken, and spider webs nearly dominated the interior. They walked cautiously inside swatting flies as they went.

She stopped at the far end of the building at the last stall on the left. She opened the gate and stepped inside. "Here's where Thunder lived," she said glancing around at the dirt floor.

"So, if we read the clue correctly, the next clue should be somewhere in here," said Spencer.

"The iron of Thunder hides the clue down under," said Madison.

They both slowly glanced at the floor.

"You know this is not top soil that we're standing on," said Spencer.

"I know exactly what we're standing on," said Madison. "I used to watch them clean this stall."

Spencer slowly looked at Madison. He frowned. "I'll get a shovel," he said.

It was nearly an hour later, when Spencer stopped and straightened his tired back. He leaned the shovel against the side of the stall.

"I didn't know anything could smell as bad as that does," said Spencer.

"City slicker," said Madison.

"I didn't notice you bent over a shovel with your nose down in it."

"That's men's work," she said.

Spencer leaned against the wall. "Let me ask you something. Why is there no such thing as women's work because it's too demeaning, yet there are things that are considered men's work?"

"Typical male response," she said. "Whine if you can't get your way."

"Typical female response," said Spencer. "Attack your opponent personally when you've obviously lost the argument."

"I didn't know we were arguing about anything."

"You would have known if you had won the argument," said Spencer.

"All right, truce," said Madison. "We're not getting any place this way. Now, it's obvious there is no clue here."

"Well, for once, I agree with you," said Spencer. "So, if it isn't buried here, where is the clue?"

"I don't know," said Madison. "I still can't believe this isn't the spot under the iron of Thunder. Everything points to this stable."

"Is this the only place left where Thunder would have spent time?"

Madison thought for a moment. "He spent as much time running around that track," she said pointing out the door.

"Well, I'm not going to dig up that entire track," said Spencer. "There must be some other place where Thunder spent his time."

"I can tell you where he has spent most of his time, and that's in his grave," said Madison.

"That's interesting, but does us no good," said Spencer.

"On the contrary," said Madison. "One of his horseshoes is implanted on his tombstone."

"Where's his grave?"

Madison pointed out the door. "Over there in that pasture."

Spencer grabbed his shovel. "Let's go."

It was a picturesque spot, the lone willow tree with the white board fence around it stood in the rolling fields of green. Tucked away under the sagging branches was a medium-sized stone with the name, Thunder, on it. A rusted horseshoe hung proudly on the face of the stone just over the name.

Spencer stuck his shovel in the mounded dirt just in front of the tombstone.

"What are you doing?" asked Madison.

"I'm digging up the second clue," said Spencer.

"You can't do that. That's desecrating a grave."

"I have to if we want to get the next clue."

"I won't have it. I don't care if the jewelry is buried there, you're not digging up Thunder."

"In the first place, it's probably just below the surface, well away from the dearly departed, and in the second place it's just a horse, expensive one, but a horse just the same."

"Just a horse!" said Madison. "Just a horse! Do you have idea how much that beautiful animal cost?"

"I wouldn't brag about it," said Spencer. "Because from where I'm standing that was money poorly spent."

Madison stomped her foot. "Damn! You can be so infuriating!"

"That's part of my charm."

"Charm! You don't even know the meaning of the word."

Spencer glanced at the grave. "Well, what do you want to do? You know the second clue is here."

She paused and stared at the grave. "How deep are you going?"

"'Til I find it."

"Don't go any lower than a foot. Okay?"

"Three feet."

"Two."

"You got it," said Spencer.

He picked up his shovel and started to dig. Nearly a foot below the surface, he hit metal. "I think I found it," he said. He fell to his knees and dug the soft dirt with his hands. He soon pulled from the ground a small dirt encrusted metal box.

"I hope the next one is as easy as that one was," said Madison.

Spencer scowled. "What was so easy about digging up an entire stable of horse manure?"

"I didn't have to do the digging."

Spencer pried open the lid and removed a scrap of paper. Inside was written the number, 1776. "We got problems," he said.

Madison leaned over. "Is that all it says?"

Spencer slowly nodded his head.

+++

It was early evening. Madison had cooked hamburgers on the grill, and they both sat down to eat. Spencer was quiet as he stared at the paper with the number, 1776.

"It's gotta be something patriotic," he said.

"Well, that certainly narrows things down," she said.

"Maybe the next clue is on the back of the Declaration of Independence."

"Been done."

Spencer smiled. "Oh, yeah."

Madison leaned back in her chair and smiled. "Aren't you at least a little bit curious about those two?"

"What two?"

"Your great grandfather and my great grandmother, Harrison and Elizabeth," said Madison. "From what we can tell, they had some kind of a relationship together. They even lived together in Harrison's house, didn't they?"

Spencer thrust the last bite of his sandwich in his mouth. "As far as I know."

Madison jumped. "I know what we can do. Harrison is still alive. We can go see him and find out first hand."

Spencer picked up both plates and set them in the sink. "Sorry, he's ninety-nine years old and out of his mind."

Madison's smile disappeared. She ran her hands through her hair. "There must be something we can do."

"This is really important to you, isn't it?" asked Spencer.

"Yes, it is. I don't know why. Must be the romantic side of me. Aren't you curious how they got together? Were they in love? What caused them to separate? Just too many unanswered questions."

Spencer yawned.

"Well, I can see we hit a nerve with you," she said.

"Just a little tired, I guess."

Madison got to her feet. "Maybe a good night's sleep would help." She started for the stairway, Spencer just behind her.

They slowly walked the stairs. Neither spoke. Madison stopped in front of her bedroom and turned to Spencer. He was smiling. It was a nervous smile that pleased Madison. He started to move his hand in her direction and quickly pulled it back.

"Well, I guess this is it...good night, that is," he said.

"Yeah, I guess so," she replied with a smile.

He leaned his head forward as if to kiss her and pulled back.

"Six o'clock okay with you?" he asked.

"Sounds perfect," she said.

Spencer put his hand into his pocket and fidgeted with his keys. "Tomorrow we'll find out what 1776 means."

"I'm looking forward to it," she said softly, almost seductively.

Spencer fidgeted with a button on his shirt and then, without warning, thrust his hand in her direction. "Well, good night."

She took his hand and lightly shook it. Still smiling, she stared into his eyes. Suddenly, Spencer relaxed. He smiled as he looked into her eyes. Their hands stilled, the grip tightened.

"Guess I should go now," he said softly.

Madison said nothing.

Spencer paused as he stared into her eyes. It was amazing how much she looked like her great grandmother. It was almost as if she was reincarnated, and yet he imagined her so much different from this woman called Madison. She must have been a woman of a gentle nature, soft and feminine, yet strong of will and conviction. Madison possessed the same beauty, but that's where the similarity ended. Yet, this woman of today had a certain charm, grace, and womanly stature that was characteristic of women who wore floor-length dresses and had gracious manners of an era long forgotten.

Spencer released his grip on her hand and stepped back. "Good night," he said, turned, and walked away. Madison watched as he opened his bedroom door and disappeared behind it.

+++

It was nearly 6:30 when Spencer stumbled into the kitchen. Madison was leaning over the stove stirring bacon that sizzled and popped. She was wearing a dress, her hair done and make up in place.

"Morning, sleepy head," she said.

"Morning."

"Coffee is done, if you don't mind pouring yourself a cup," she said, removing the bacon from the skillet and placing it on a folded paper towel. She held up two eggs. "Scrambled?"

"That's fine," said Spencer grabbing the coffeepot. He poured a cup and took a seat at the table. "Is there anything I can do to help?"

"Not a thing," she said. "The eggs are almost done. I've already eaten."

"Tomorrow morning I'm fixing breakfast," said Spencer. "How do you feel about pop tarts?"

Madison laughed. "Don't worry about it. I've loved to cook since I was a child. Unfortunately, I love to eat as well."

"Doesn't show," said Spencer.

Madison stopped and smiled at Spencer. "Why, Mr. Ellington, that almost sounded like a compliment."

Spencer blushed. "Well, in a way…"

"I never thought I could ever compete with Elizabeth," she said as she set a plate of food in front of Spencer.

"It was different with your great grandmother," said Spencer stabbing his eggs with a fork. "All I had was a photograph of this incredibly beautiful woman. Her personality, style, and grace, I invented myself. I molded her into the ideal woman, the quintessential goddess found only in dreams."

Madison took a seat across from Spencer. "You don't think that such a woman exists in real life, do you?"

"Not hardly," said Spencer. "No one is that perfect."

"You have a low regard for women, don't you?" said Madison, her lips set in a thin line.

"On the contrary, I have the utmost regard for women," he said. "In fact, I consider my mother to be the model that God designed for the rest of us to follow."

"But as equals in the business world…"

Spencer dropped his fork. "You know if you want to debate women's rights, you need to find some beer-swilling, wife-beating redneck. I'm not interested. What's with you, anyway? You seem to be spoiling for a fight."

Madison grew quiet. Her face softened. "I'm sorry," she muttered. "It's just that no man has ever taken me seriously."

"Give me a chance, will you?"

Madison said nothing.

"Please," he said.

She smiled and looked away. "I guess I can try to get this chip off my shoulder."

Spencer finished his breakfast and sipped his coffee. "So how did you sleep last night? Any dreams to lead us to the 1776?"

"Oh, I had a dream, all right," she said. "But I don't think it will help us find 1776. I dreamed about letters...tons of letters. Every time I would open a mailbox, hundreds of letters would fall out."

"Were they addressed to you?"

"I don't know. I never saw the addresses. Wonder what it means?"

Spencer jumped to his feet. "I know exactly what it means." He opened the back door. "I'll be right back."

Spencer returned and dropped a box on the kitchen table. He opened the flaps and pulled out bundles of letters. "Here's where your dream was taking you."

Madison picked up one of the letters. It had yellowed and was brittle with age. "Where did you get these?"

"Grandpa Harrison asked me to destroy them," he said, picking up one of the letters. "Look who he was writing to."

Madison turned over one of the envelopes. "He was writing to Elizabeth." She sifted through the pile and found another. "Here's one that she wrote to him. Wonder what separated them."

"Look at grandpa's address," said Spencer. "That's a military base in England, and the date is July 10, 1914. That's the time of the First World War."

"So, they were in love, and he had to go off to war. How romantic," she said.

"What's so romantic about going to fight in a war?"

"Not that, you boob," she said. "It's the fact that they were in love and were forced to separate." Spencer shrugged his shoulders. "Doesn't it make you the least bit curious as to how they met, how long were they together, or why they never got married? These are all questions that need to be answered."

"The only question that needs to be answered is what does 1776 mean," he said.

"Oh, that can wait."

"I'm glad you think so."

"Right now, we need to organize these letters," she said, pulling them from the box. "You take your great grandpa's letters, and I'll take Elizabeth's and we'll arrange them chronologically from the earliest date to the last."

They both began by sorting through the letters, reading the faded dates on the envelopes as best they could and stacking them in neat piles on the table.

Madison picked the letter on top and opened it. "This is grandma's first letter to Harrison, and it's dated June 18, 1914," she said looking up at Spencer. "What's the date of your first one? It must be before this one, otherwise she wouldn't have had an address."

"April 27, 1914."

"Assuming she wrote him back the day she received his, that makes it over six weeks for his letter to get here."

"They didn't exactly have overnight service in those days," said Spencer.

"Okay, you go first," said Madison. "You read what Harrison had to say in his first letter to Elizabeth."

Spencer carefully opened the envelope and removed the brittle paper inside. He held up two small pieces of paper. "A man of few words."

"Just read what he had to say," said Madison, her voice tinged with excitement.

Spencer began to read, "Arrived here safely. Don't know how, though. German submarine took a shot at us with one of them torpedoes. Dang thing slid right under our boat. Bernie, a guy I met on the way over here, said they had it set too low in the water. Guess that proves you don't have to worry none. Somebody's looking out for me."

"Don't know how long we're going to be here, or for that matter, where we're going from here. They keep things like that a secret from us privates. Can't say as I blame them. There are some real unsavory characters in this lot. Suppose it's possible there could be a spy among them. Bernie is a good guy, though. He's a preacher back in a small town in Ohio. He's got five kids. Seems like he needs to find a hobby or something."

"Ain't going to get mushy with you. No telling who all is going to read this before it gets to you. After all, I am a soldier, and soldiers don't let on how much they miss their women."

"Got to go. We're going on a five-mile hike, and I haven't even stowed my gear. Will write when I can."

Spencer flipped the last page over and then back. "He didn't even sign it."

Madison carefully unfolded her letter and began to read,

"My dearest Harrison,

Watching you leave me was one of the hardest things I've ever done. I miss you so much. My heart aches every minute of the day. They tell me someone will probably read this before you see it, but I don't care. I don't mind if the whole world knows how much I love you."

"Seems so funny. The year and a half we spent together seemed to fly by, and now I stare at the clock watching the minutes go by. One minute seems like an hour now that you're gone from me. I wish I could go to sleep and wake up years from now, and you would be back here with me where you belong."

Madison grew silent. She continued to read the letter, wiping her eyes and sniffling. "My heart aches for her," she said.

Spencer glanced at the stacks of letters. "You're not going to be like this with every letter, are you?"

She pulled a tissue from her purse and blew her nose. "You just wouldn't understand."

Spencer leafed through the letters. "Let's jump ahead to next month and see how Harrison is doing." He picked a letter and pulled it from the pile. He began to read.

"Got a letter from you today. Can't tell you how much that meant to hear from you. Sure do miss you. Miss being home as well. These English people over here are nice to us, but they sure are a lot different from Americans. I've come to the conclusion there ain't nothing like America and the people who live there."

"I know you're probably worried about me over here by myself and all the girls over here. Just wanted you to know you got nothing to worry about. We had some free time the other day and a bunch of guys were going into town, if you get what I mean. I told them I had a girl back home. They laughed a lot and called me names, but I stayed at camp just the same. I think I told you about Bernie, he's my best friend. He kind of felt sorry for me and stayed behind as well. They don't make better friends than Bernie."

"Still don't know what's going to happen to us. We train for combat every day. To tell you the truth, I'd just as soon we get on with it. The waiting is killing me, and I'm sick to death of pretend fighting. Rumor has it we'll be going to France. Seems that's where the fighting is. Makes you wonder how these things get started. I suppose some big shot says something that another big shot doesn't like, and away we go. Wouldn't mind it so much if the big shots would fight it out, but unfortunately, the little guys like me have to clean up the mess."

"Well, got to go now. It's time for us to go eat. I understand now why the Army calls it mess. When I get home, I hope I never see another baked bean in my life. They haven't started serving them for breakfast yet, but I'm sure it's coming."

"We have to go see your grandpa Harrison," said Madison. "There are so many questions I have to ask him."

"It'll do no good," said Spencer. "He's out of his head most all the time. Besides, we need to discover the meaning of 1776."

"Let's go see Uncle Bradley. He can help."

"What about the jewelry?"

Madison jumped to her feet. "Are you driving or am I?"

 # CHAPTER SEVENTEEN

It was after nine in the morning when Spencer and Madison found their way down the hall of the nursing home. They turned the corner to her uncle's room to find him sitting upright in a wheelchair.

"How are you, Uncle Bradley?" asked Madison.

"Never better," he said. "In fact, I think I'll find old man Fogerty and see if he wants to race wheelchairs."

Bradley extended his hand to Spencer. "Good morning, young man, and how are you?"

"Fine, sir," he said, taking the old man's hand.

Madison took a seat beside Bradley. "I have a few questions for you."

"If it's about the clues, I've told you all I can," said Bradley.

"Not exactly, but I have to tell you, we got the first one with no trouble at all," she said.

"Figured you would," he said. "That first one was to get you warmed up. They get tougher as they go."

Madison smiled. "You did the work on these clues, didn't you?"

"Pretty much, but it was Elizabeth's idea."

"Why, Uncle Bradley?" she asked. "Please tell me why she wanted us to jump through all these hoops?"

"Oh, I wish I could, but like I told you before, I'm sworn to secrecy," said Bradley. "But let me tell you one thing I don't think you realize. Do you remember how you two got along before? How are you guys doing now?"

Madison turned to Spencer and then back to Bradley. "So, this was about pulling us together. A common goal uniting enemies kind of thing."

Bradley smiled, but said nothing.

"We still hate each other," she said. "But we have progressed to the point where we don't spit on each other."

"Progress is sometimes measured in small amounts," said Bradley.

"Uncle Bradley, we came here to ask you about Elizabeth and Harrison."

"I'll tell you whatever I can remember, but it isn't much," said Bradley. "It was a long time ago, and I was just a boy."

"First of all, you mentioned that you did not know where Harrison went. As far as you were concerned, he simply disappeared. Well, we've been piecing things together from some old letters, and it seems he either joined the Army or was drafted. All we know is that he was suddenly at a military base in England."

Bradley slowly nodded his head. "That makes sense."

"What I'd like to learn from you, is how they met," said Madison. "She gets off the Titanic, doesn't know a soul and somehow meets Harrison."

"Well, you've got it right so far," said Bradley. "I don't remember all the details. We'd been here for several days, just kind of wandering around. Mama tried getting a job, but had no success. I just remember wanting something to eat and a place to lay down. Now mind you, this was the middle of April in New York City, and it was cold, very cold. It seemed like it snowed every day that winter."

"Then it happened. We were standing on a street corner waiting to cross, when this big, beautiful car pulled over. The driver opened the door and asked if we wanted a ride. Now I had never been in a car, much less gone for a ride. We stood there for what seemed like forever, just standing there, and him a holding that door open. The cold and hunger must have finally gotten to her because the next thing I knew we were inside that beautiful car on our way down the road."

"I remember thinking what a nice man Harrison was, even that first day I met him. He asked us where we were going. Mama tried to lie to him, tried to convince him we were on our way home, but he saw right through it. He figured right away that we had no place to go. Next thing I knew, he was inviting us over to his house and offering mama a job as a housekeeper. To this day, I don't know whether he was just that nice of a guy or whether he fell in love with her right from the start. Either way, we had a roof over our heads and something to eat."

"So what you're saying is that you're not sure if they fell in love right away," said Madison.

Bradley leaned back in his chair and smiled. His eyes lost their focus and seemed to wander. "Their relationship was like no other since Adam and Eve, and if it wasn't right away, it was within weeks. You know, when a man is in love, truly in love, he has a smile just for her that cannot be faked, duplicated, or mistaken. Harrison had a smile for her that spoke volumes, and yet it said very simply that he loved her with all his heart, and he yearned to be with her."

"Why didn't they get married?" asked Spencer.

"You have to remember that they were only together for a year or so before he took off. To tell you the truth, I'm surprised they didn't."

"What was it like back then, Uncle Bradley?" asked Madison.

"You want to know what it was like before computers, paved roads, indoor plumbing, and television? It was great. Mind you now, it all happened in my lifetime. When you think about it, the twentieth century was truly the most incredible era in the history of mankind. Prior to the 1900's, man had advanced to riding on horses and cooking over an open fire. With the dawn of the twentieth century came a revolution of sorts. One invention followed another, and before you knew it, we were watching TV and walking on the moon.

"Harrison was smart enough to recognize what was going on and decided to jump on the bandwagon, as they say. He invented some kind of a part for automobiles and started his own manufacturing plant. By the time he met Elizabeth, he was already fairly wealthy and making plans for the future. I think the timing was right for him to meet Mama and to fall in love."

"How did he treat you?" Madison asked.

"Like the father I never had," said Bradley. "He was the kindest most wonderful man I've ever known. Harrison and I had a special handshake that only he and I knew about. We would put our right hands back-to-back, slide them away from each other, and then shake hands. He always said that was our special handshake and that I was to keep it a secret. We developed a bond between us, the likes I've never known."

"What were Harrison and Elizabeth like together?" asked Madison.

"One day, we were on a picnic…now that I think about it, it seemed as if we were always on a picnic. Anyway, when we had finished, Harrison decided to take us for a ride down the river in a canoe. I remember he loved canoes, in fact he did it all himself, didn't need any help. We were drifting along so quietly, but unbeknownst to us, there was a huge rainstorm up river. Suddenly, we were caught in a flash flood, overturning the canoe and spilling us into the raging river. I hung onto the sides of the canoe, but unfortunately, the swirling water swept Elizabeth under the surface.

"Harrison took one look at me, and I think he sensed that I would be okay. He then dove underwater searching for mama. By the time he found her, she was already near the shore. He grabbed her and helped onto the shore and then turned to me. By that time, I was nearly a half-mile down river and picking up speed all the time. I don't mind telling you I was scared to death."

"My God, Uncle Bradley, what happened?"

"Fortunately, the canoe got hung up on a rock giving Harrison enough time to save me. That night when we sat down to eat, I remember Harrison told us that we always had a place to stay at his house. That afternoon's scare had shown him how much we meant to him. Secretly, I think he was telling mama how much he loved her. I never forgot that day…guess I never will."

Bradley shook his head as if coming out of a trance. "And you say Harrison is still alive. Must be over a hundred years old."

"He turns a hundred this year," said Spencer.

"Isn't that funny. Years ago, eleven years difference in our ages was a big deal. Today, it hardly means a thing. We're both simply old men." He ran his hand through the thin, white hair on his head. "Damn, I sure wish I could see him once more."

"Uncle Bradley, can you think of anything else about those two?" asked Madison.

He glanced at the floor. "I'm sorry. It was such a long time ago."

Madison got to her feet, and Spencer followed. "You've been a great help," she said. "We know a lot more now than we did before."

"Tell me," said Bradley. "Why the sudden interest in a love affair that happened so many years ago?"

Madison paused. "I don't know for sure. I just know it's something I must do."

"Well, good luck with your quest," said Bradley.

They turned to the door. "Thanks again, Uncle Bradley," she said. "We'll see you again real soon."

+++

It was early evening. Spencer brought a bag of burgers and fries to the table. They both slid stacks of letters to one end to make room.

"I think we should read another batch of letters while we eat," said Madison as she unwrapped her sandwich.

"I think we should figure out what 1776 means," said Spencer.

"There's no way we're going to figure out a clue from 1776," she said. She sifted through the stacks of letters. "Besides, the real mystery is right here in front of us."

Spencer pulled a piece of paper from his pocket and stared at the 1776 written on it. "I don't think it's that hard."

Madison opened one of the letters. "Here's one written by Elizabeth shortly before Christmas."

Spencer started to open one of the letters, stopped and threw it back down. "Somehow, reading these letters just doesn't feel right, especially since he asked me to destroy them."

She ignored his remark and began to read,

"My dearest Harrison,

I didn't think it was possible for me to last this long without you. I know you're doing this for your country and you have no choice, but I can't help my feelings"

Spencer raised a hand as if he were stopping traffic. "Can we skip the intimate details and just go for the meat?"

"You're so romantic," she said, continuing to read silently. She read the first and second pages, turned to the third page and began to read aloud,

"Bradley and I picked out a Christmas tree today. I think you would have liked it. As I was searching through the trees, I allowed myself the pleasure of imagining you coming home to see it. I guess that's why I spent so much time looking for just the right one. I want this Christmas to be perfect, just in case my dream does come true. I can't imagine that God would stand by another day and allow my heart to ache this much. I pray every night that He will send you home to me. I know I'm being selfish, but I can't help this emptiness inside. You see, my love, I am convinced that God brought us together. Think about it. The bizarre events that brought us together could not have happened as they did by mere chance. It is by the hand of God that joined us, and I will always be grateful."

"As I said before, this will be the most perfect Christmas. I have already wrapped your presents. I wouldn't want you to come home and discover what Bradley and I got you."

Madison continued reading the letter, but silently to herself.

"You know, when I said something about getting to the meat, I meant information not more I miss you's," said Spencer.

"You know you don't have a romantic bone in your body," she said.

"Yes, I do."

"No, you don't."

"I sympathize with the woman, and I feel sorry for her. I really do. It's just that we've been over that ground. What else can we learn from her letters?"

Madison crossed her legs and leaned back. "This woman is pouring her heart out, and you're wondering what you can learn from her letters?"

"You make it sound as if I don't care," he said. "Don't forget, I'm the one who fell in love with a photo of a woman who lived decades ago."

Madison jumped in her seat. "You know what we need to do now? We need to go see your great grandfather, Harrison. My God, why didn't I think of this before? Here we have one of the key players still alive. He can explain to us what happened."

"Won't do you any good," said Spencer.

"Why?"

"He's out of his head most of the time."

"But he is thinking clearly, some of the time?"

"Oh, yes, indeed," said Spencer.

"Then let's take the chance."

"It's a long drive up there."

"Not anymore," she said as she started to walk. "My company has a corporate jet."

Two phone calls later, Spencer found himself aboard a small Lear jet cruising high over the farmlands of the

Midwest. After landing at Metro Airport in Detroit, a black limousine whisked them off to the hospital.

The hallway was crowded as they made their way to Harrison's room. Harrison was lying on his back babbling softly. Spencer and Madison walked slowly across the room and stopped at his bedside. He was talking aloud to no one in particular. His eyes were distant, glassed over with no life in them.

Harrison slowly turned his head in their direction, his eyes focusing on his two visitors. Suddenly, his face turned sullen as he stared at Madison. His head reared slightly from the pillow as he studied her face. Madison nervously stepped back. It was as if he recognized her, but was unsure what to say or do.

"Is he okay?" she asked.

"I don't know," said Spencer. "I've never seen him like this. It's as if he knows you."

Then, his face softened, and he settled his head back down on his pillow. A smile broke out on his face. "Hi, Liz," he said. "I knew you'd come back to me."

Madison glanced at Spencer. "He thinks I'm Elizabeth."

Spencer leaned over the bed. "Grandpa, I'd like you to meet my friend, Madison."

Harrison's smile didn't change. His eyes remained focused on Madison. "It's been so long since I've seen you. Oh, it's been nice over the past few years when you would come to visit me, but I couldn't see your face. I missed seeing you so much. Oh, I could tell when you were here in the room. You know how I could tell? I could smell you. You always had a fragrance of spring blossoms. That's how I could tell you were here. You couldn't fool me."

"Grandpa, this is Madison. She is Elizabeth's great granddaughter," said Spencer.

Harrison reached out with his tired, weathered hand. Madison glanced down and gently placed her hand in his. "You know, it was more than just a smell that told me you were here with me. It was a feeling, a feeling unlike any other feeling in the world. When two people who love each other as much as you and I do, death can't keep us apart It might keep me from seeing you, but it doesn't stop the feeling, I never lost the feeling, all the time you've been gone."

"Grandpa, we came here to ask you a few questions," said Spencer.

"We had one Christmas together," said Harrison. "Still have the watch you gave me. Treasure it more than life itself."

"Suppose we should go," said Spencer. "This doesn't appear to be a good day."

Madison leaned over the bed. "Harrison, we came here to find out why you never married Elizabeth," she shouted.

The smile on his face disappeared. Very quietly, he said, "You know why."

"I forgot. Tell me again."

Harrison stared intently at Madison. His grip tightened around her hand.

"There's a warm glow that dominates the very soul of every man or woman who is in love. If you've never been in love, you wouldn't know what I'm talking about, but to those who are, you know exactly what I mean. The warm glow is always there even in times of trouble. Anger, jealousy, fright, these are all emotions that will come and go, but the embers of love will never go away. I carried that warm glow for you. I carried it even through the bad times. I have it still today."

Madison glanced at Spencer. "This is what is known as true love."

"Come on," said Spencer. "We'll come back another day."

The next morning, Spencer picked up a scrap of paper and pushed back from the breakfast table.

"1776," he read aloud. "We need to get back on the scent of the jewelry."

"Spoken like a true man," said Madison, sitting down at the table.

"Now what?"

"We're on the trail of discovering what happened to a relationship between your great grandfather and my great grandmother, and you want to go searching for jewelry."

"Yeah, silly me," said Spencer. "Searching for the jewelry would only make me incredibly rich. Why would I want to do something as crazy as that?"

"You don't have a sensitive bone in your body, do you?"

"I consider myself a very sensitive man," he said. "You may remember I was the one who fell in love with a picture of your great grandmother."

"Actually, I'm not sure if that's a sign of a sensitive guy or a sign that you're sick."

"Either way, we need to figure out what 1776 means," said Spencer.

Madison slid her chair back from the table. "Sounds American, sounds patriotic, sounds like I don't have a clue."

"Is there a flag in the family, one that goes back a long time?" asked Spencer.

"Not that I know of," she said. "Why?"

"I was thinking the number of stars on the flag would depend on how old it was, and that might mean something."

"Nice thought, but there's no flag," she said.

Spencer pointed his finger in her direction. "I've got it! For years, they've made reproductions of the Declaration of Independence, old wrinkled paper and everything. Do you remember one of those in the house somewhere?"

"That sounds familiar. Why?"

"Since the original was written in 1776, I'm thinking there might be a clue on your copy."

"I don't know where to begin looking for it," she said. "Kind of a long shot anyhow, isn't it?"

"Got any better ideas?"

Madison stared at the stacks of letters piled on the table. "I'd rather read these to find out what happened all those years ago."

Spencer picked one up and stared at the envelope. "Wonder if this stamp is worth anything," he muttered. "This letter is dated August 15, 1915." A pile of mail was on the table as well, and Spencer picked up a credit card application addressed to Uncle Bradley.

"You know that's typical of you," she said. "I look at these letters as a source of information for finding out what happened to these two people. You look at them and wonder if you can make a buck from the…"

Spencer jumped. "That's it!" he shouted, still staring at the envelope in his hand. "1776! What's the address here at this house?"

"You know what it is. It's right there in front of you."

"1774 Windsor Street," said Spencer. "You must have a 1776 Windsor."

"Old man Blankenship lives next door. Uncle Bradley hates his guts," she said.

"Let's go," said Spencer. He led Madison out the door and onto the sidewalk in front of the houses. He pointed at the house next door. "Is that where this Blankenship guy lives?"

"That's his house," she said.

Spencer pointed at a small sign near his front door that read, 1776 Windsor. "There's the answer to the 1776 riddle."

Madison smiled. "You might be right," she said. "But how are we going to get old man Blankenship to let us search his house?"

"We don't have to search his house," said Spencer.

"How are we going to find it if we don't go through his house?"

Spencer pointed again at the sign. "It's there, behind the address sign."

"Do you really think so?"

"I'm sure of it."

"So how do we get it?"

Spencer walked across the lawn and stood at the boundary between the two houses. He studied the sign as if he could see through it. "The way I see it, we have two choices. We can wait until after dark, or we can distract him by having you walk around in the backyard in the nude while I slip up to the front porch."

Spencer started across the neighbor's lawn. "Follow me."

Madison fell in behind him. "Where are we going?" she asked.

"We're going to ask him if we can look behind his sign," he said.

She slowly shook her head. "He isn't going to like it."

Spencer stepped onto the porch and rang the doorbell. "I'm sure he's a reasonable man. Once I explain our situation, he will be more than happy to help us out."

The front door swung open, and an old man with a grizzled beard and dark gray clothes stood behind the screen. "If you're a salesman, consider yourself lucky that I'm out of ammunition."

Spencer pointed at Madison who by now was just stepping onto the porch. "This is Madison. Her uncle lives next door."

"Who the hell are you?" barked the old man.

"My name is Spencer Ellington. I am a friend of the family, and your name is…"

"If you're not selling anything, what the hell do you want?"

Spencer paused. "There's a program in the neighborhood for replacing old address signs on the front of houses. With your permission, we will at no charge to you replace this old faded sign with a brand-new vinyl plaque with your address numbers on it."

"Don't want a new sign," he said and slammed the door shut.

Spencer lightly rapped on the door. It opened just enough for the old man to look out.

"You're still here?" he asked.

"Okay, I wasn't exactly honest with you," said Spencer. "I'm from the fire department, and there are laws regarding address signs. You see, we have to be able to find your…"

"Tell your buddies to let it burn to the ground. Insurance is paid, and I hate the God damn place anyhow," he said and closed the door again.

Spencer tapped twice, and the door swung open. The old man stood in the doorway with a scowl on his face.

"You've been lying to me again, haven't you?" he asked.

Spencer blushed. "Well, kinda."

"What the hell do you want?" asked the old man. "And try telling the truth for a change."

"I want to look behind your address sign."

"Why?"

"I think there's a message for us hidden behind it."

"I don't want you tearing down my sign. I like it just the way it is."

"I'll pay you money."

"I don't need money. I have all that I need."

Spencer turned to Madison. "This woman here said she would walk around in her backyard in the nude if you let us look under your sign."

Madison frowned. "Spencer!"

The old man smiled. "Have you discussed this with her, because from where I stand, she ain't taking to the idea."

"Sorry for my friend's disgraceful sense of humor, Mr. Blankenship," she said taking a few steps closer.

"Well, I guess that about does it," said Spencer. "If we can't get permission to look behind that sign, we're all through."

The old man smiled and then broke out into laughter. "Go ahead and help yourself to the sign," he said. "Your Uncle Bradley told me you'd probably be around to see me."

"Well, why did you tell me before that we couldn't remove the sign?" Spencer asked.

"Just kidding around," he said. "I know you didn't think it was funny, but I sure did." He started to close the door, then reopened it. "You be damn careful with that sign now, you hear?"

"Oh, yes sir," said Spencer. "I'm going to get some tools right now."

The old man laughed. "Just pullin' your chain again," he said. He disappeared into the house and returned with a crowbar and hammer. "Here, tear the nasty thing off the wall. It looks like shit. I bought a new one when I heard that you guys would be coming around."

"Thanks, Mr. Blankenship," said Spencer.

"Don't mention it," he said and closed the door.

"We're back in business," said Spencer. He eased the end of the crowbar under wooden sign and pried. The wood snapped in half. "Hope he wasn't kidding about getting a new sign." He pulled off the rest of the wood and threw it on the porch floor.

"Now what?" said Spencer, staring at the brick wall.

Madison stepped closer and lightly ran her hand over the brick. "I thought you said it would be under the sign," she said.

"I would have bet the farm that…"

The front door opened slightly, and the old man stuck his arm out pointing at the wood lying on the floor. "It's down there on the back of the sign, dumb ass!"

Spencer turned to the pile of wood on the floor. There stuck to the back of one of the boards was a yellowed envelope. He picked it up and opened it to find a key and a folded piece of paper. He carefully unfolded the scrap of brittle paper.

"It's another clue," he said. "I wonder how many of these there are."

"What does it say?" asked Madison.

Spencer read aloud, "Through the tapestry rose the key fits and opens a world you'll want to visit."

"All we have to do is figure out what a tapestry rose is," said Madison.

"Aren't those tapestries piled up in your living room?"

"Uncle Bradley loved tapestries and had them hanging all over the house. When the house got broken into, they tore them all down."

Spencer jumped off the porch. "Come on. Let's go find the tapestry rose."

There were over twenty tapestries stacked neatly in a pile in the corner of the living room. Spencer stared at the one on top. It was a seventeenth century scene inspired by the paintings of Francois Boucher. It was an Italian tapestry portraying a picturesque scene of the European countryside.

"Never seen so many fancy rugs," said Spencer.

"These are tapestries, you idiot," said Madison. "Expensive and rare works of art."

"I was just kidding you," said Spencer.

"No, you weren't," she said. "You barely know how to eat with utensils, so it would come as no surprise to me if you considered these priceless tapestries to be rugs."

Spencer stepped closer to Madison. "You know, just because you have money doesn't make you the queen of culture."

"I have more culture in my little finger, than you will ever have in your whole body."

"Says who?"

"Says me."

"Says you?"

"That's right. Says me."

Spencer ran his fingers through his hair. "Damn, you're a spoiled brat," he said.

Madison leaned over and picked up one corner of the first tapestry. "Grab that end. What do you say we find the rose?"

Spencer smiled as he picked up the other end and swung the tapestry from the pile.

They were nearly halfway through the pile when they came across one of a woman sitting in a chair and holding a single rose in her hand.

"That's it!" said Spencer. "There's our rose." He bent over and studied the material. "I still don't see how the key is suppose to slip through the fabric."

"Turn it over," said Madison.

"What do you mean?"

"If there is an opening, it will be easier to see on the back."

Spencer flipped that part of the tapestry over. He carefully examined the area on the backside of the rose. "There it is. It's a small slit in the fabric just big enough for a key."

"We did it," said Madison.

Spencer got to his feet. The smile disappeared from his face as he scanned the room. "Not really," he said. "Because now we have to figure out where it once belonged."

Madison's eyes slowly scanned the room. "Oops."

"Yeah, oops," he said. "Can you remember where it once hung?"

Madison walked across the room and studied the wall. Faded paint created an outline where a tapestry once hung, and there were nails in the wall near the ceiling that once held the weight of fabric. She slowly walked the rest of the room. "Looks like there were four of them in this room alone," she said.

"But we still don't know where each of them goes," said Spencer.

"There is one way to find out," she said. "We can go through the family pictures. There's bound to be one that shows it in the background."

"Let's go," said Spencer.

+++

It was just a little after dark when Spencer and Madison finished their dinner. It had been a day of searching through boxes of photographs with no success. They had found many pictures of the inside of the house, some showing a few of the tapestries hanging in the background, but they could not find one that showed the girl with the rose.

Spencer pushed back from the table and leaned back. "Well, if nothing else, I now know your family. That was more pictures than I thought possible."

"I still can't believe there was not one photograph that could help," she said.

"Did you realize that we know nothing about your great grandmother before she came to America?" said Spencer. "My brother is a cop, and he thinks she's a thief."

Madison sat up in her chair. "Why would he think that?"

"Well, look at it this way," said Spencer with a smile. "She came to America on the Titanic third class, and yet she had with her some of the most expensive jewelry in the world. It just doesn't fit."

"That doesn't make her a thief," said Madison.

"Maybe not, but it does make you wonder," he said.

Madison pointed at the pile of letters. "The answer could be right there. There are so many things we don't know about those two. For example, they lived together for a year or two. Wasn't that a little risqué for back then? And if they did live together, was there any hanky-panky involved?"

"We live together, and there's no hanky-panky involved," said Spencer.

"I've noticed that not once have you tried anything," she said. "I don't know whether to be impressed or insulted."

"I thought you still hated me."

"What gave you that impression?"

"Oh, I don't know. Setting fire to your car and tearing your dress from your body with my car were clues that I wasn't scoring points with you."

"You're lucky you're still alive," she said.

Spencer got to his feet and stretched. "What do you say we get to bed and get an early start tomorrow?"

Madison got up and started for the kitchen. "You go ahead, and I'll catch up in a minute." She walked across the kitchen and piled dirty dishes in the sink. She put food in the refrigerator, wiped off the countertops, and turned off the lights. She walked back into the living room to find Spencer waiting for her.

"I thought you were going to bed," she said.

Spencer smiled. "Oh, I just thought I'd walk you to your room."

"Well, that was sweet of you," she said, as she started up the stairs. "I guess I'd forgotten that men can be nice at times."

"We're not all bad all the time," he said. "We just sometimes forget about women's needs."

"Women's needs? I know I've never heard a man say those words."

They stopped in front of Madison's bedroom.

"No, really," she said. "Why did you wait for me?"

"I've been thinking," said Spencer. "I fell madly in love with a woman I could never have, and here is her great granddaughter who is just as beautiful and, I'm sure, just as intelligent."

Madison smiled. "Well, on behalf of my great grandmother and me, we thank you for the flattering comment."

"I know I have no business saying this, because I know I'm not in your league, but you're a beautiful and wonderful woman and I'm a lucky guy just to know you."

"Thanks, Spencer," she said. "That's very kind of you to say."

Spencer paused for a moment, then turned to leave. "Guess I should get to bed."

"What's your hurry?" she asked.

He stopped and turned. "I just thought you would want to…"

Madison stepped over to Spencer and lightly kissed him on the lips.

Spencer took her in his arms and passionately kissed her, her mouth opening as he did. His tongue slipped inside her mouth. His pulse quickened, his chest heaved. He backed her against the wall and pressed his body to hers. She moaned as her legs opened wide.

Spencer groped for the bedroom door and opened it. The two of them disappeared behind it.

+++

It was early the next morning. The morning light filtered through the slats of the blinds over the windows. Spencer and Madison lay next to each other on one side of the bed, when suddenly she screamed and sat up in bed. Spencer jumped and sat up as well. Her face was distraught, and she was gasping for breath.

"Are you okay?" he asked.

"I don't know," she said, still out of breath.

"Let me guess. You had a dream."

She rolled out of bed and put her face in her hands. "A dream I could handle. This was the worst nightmare I ever had."

"Did it have anything to do with a sinking ship?" Spencer asked.

"How did you know?"

"Am I under a locked iron grate, and water is swirling to the top?"

"I looked everywhere for something to break the lock," she said.

"Welcome to my world," said Spencer. "I knew you could catch a cold from other people, but I didn't know you could catch dreams."

"My God, it seemed so real."

"Are you okay now?"

She smiled and kissed him on the cheek. "I'm just happy to see you above water."

Spencer got out of bed and slipped on his pants. "The dream seems to haunt me, and now it has invaded your sleep."

"I wonder what it means."

"I don't know," said Spencer. "But I'll never take a bath again."

She smiled and lightly kissed him. "Thanks for last night."

"Trust me, it was my pleasure."

Madison wrapped herself in a robe and started for the door. "Let's go downstairs, and I'll fix us some breakfast."

Spencer raced across the room and stopped her at the door. He took her hands in his. "Last night was one of the most beautiful experiences of my life," he said. "I just wanted you to know that."

She smiled and lightly kissed him on the lips. "I'm so sorry to ruin it with this dream nonsense. We should be lying in bed basking in the afterglow."

Spencer took her hands in his. "I'm the one who should be apologizing. If it weren't for me, you wouldn't have had the nightmare."

Madison smiled. "Let's go have some breakfast."

"Need any help?"

She kissed him again. "Not a chance. You go sit in the living room until I'm done."

It was a dark, cavernous living room with dark stained woodwork. The walls were covered with faded wallpaper of flowered design. The only light was from two reading lamps on opposite sides of the room. The dark ceilings were ten feet from the floor, and at one end was a stone hearth fireplace with burnt residue in and around the opening.

Spencer walked casually over to one of the huge lifelike portraits that hung on every wall. It was a perfect image of Elizabeth sitting in a chair. He stepped closer to examine the print. She was sitting with her legs to one side. Her left hand rested in her lap, while the other was open and outstretched as if pointing. Spencer lightly touched the surface of the painting. There were tiny stress cracks wandering across the surface, and the once vivid colors had faded into a nearly washed out black and white appearance.

Spencer reached up and lightly touched the face of the woman in the portrait. He had fallen in love with her from the first time he saw her picture, but it was more than that. There was something about this particular portrait that seemed to captivate him, and he couldn't explain what it was. It was simple enough. Just a woman sitting in a chair, but there was more to it than that. He had a feeling about this work of art, the same kind of feeling he had when he saw the photograph of her standing on the deck of the Titanic. There was a message for him in this portrait. He was sure of that. And it was his job to figure out what this woman of long ago was trying to tell him.

Spencer stepped back from the portrait and turned towards the kitchen. "This portrait of Elizabeth, has it always been in this same spot on the wall?"

Madison came out of the kitchen wiping her hands on a dishcloth. "As far as I know. Why?"

"It's an absolutely captivating picture, and I want to know more about it."

She walked over and put her arm around him. "I swear you think more of my dead great grandmother than you do of me."

Spencer smiled. "Well, she's got more going for herself than you do."

"And what might that be?"

"She has the same incredible beauty, but she doesn't talk all the time."

Madison stepped back. "Oh, are you saying I talk too much?"

"Is that what I said? I'm sure I meant something else."

She sneered at him. "And this is the way you talk to the one who fixed you breakfast," she said. "Come on, breakfast is ready."

Arm-in-arm, they walked into the kitchen. On the table were two plates of pancakes, sausage, and a cup of coffee. They both sat down and began to eat.

"Great pancakes," said Spencer, stuffing food into his mouth.

"I'm sorry, I shouldn't respond since I talk too much," she said.

"Might have put my foot in my mouth on that one," he said.

"Might have."

Spencer sipped his coffee. "Now you can see why I'm divorced. I was always saying the wrong things."

"All you men are guilty of that," she said, taking a bite of her food.

"Maybe, and maybe not."

"What are you talking about?" she asked.

"Men don't have snits about what another man says, it's always women who get their noses out of joint over what someone says."

"And what's that supposed to mean?"

"Maybe women are too sensitive."

Madison sat up in her chair. "Maybe men are insensitive," she said. "Did you ever think of that? Typical male response to a problem, it's always the woman's fault. I'd like to have a nickel for every time women get accused of something that isn't their fault. You know, I have a mind to…"

She looked up to see Spencer smiling. "I'm proving your point, aren't I?"

Spencer slowly nodded his head.

"Okay, let's change the subject," she said.

Spencer set down his fork. "I have a feeling about the portrait of Elizabeth."

"I don't think I want to hear this."

"I think she's trying to tell us something again."

"Aren't you getting a little carried away?"

"Maybe so. I don't know."

"I'll admit, the two photos of her on the deck of the Titanic were impressive, but this is different. There's nothing unusual about this."

Spencer got to his feet. "Follow me," he said, starting for the living room. He slowed his step and lowered his voice as he entered the room and stopped in front of the painting. "This is one of the finest works of art I've ever seen."

Madison put her hands on her hips as she glanced at the painting. "Granted it's a fine piece of artwork, but I don't see anything unusual about it. And I certainly don't see any message in it."

Spencer's eyes were fixed on the painting. "There is a message in it somewhere. I can feel it."

"And the message is from my great grandmother. Did she just recently put the message in the painting?"

"I think it's been there all the time."

Madison stepped closer until she was standing next to Spencer. She silently studied the painting. "I think you're crazy."

"That could very well be, but for now, I think I'm on the right track."

"I still don't see anything unusual about it."

Spencer took one step backwards. "Often times, it's not what we see, but rather what we don't see."

"Huh?"

"Where was she when she posed for this portrait?"

Madison pointed across the room. "She was sitting right over there against that wall. As you can see, around that corner is the hallway."

Spencer grabbed a chair from the nearby dining room and set it against the wall. "Have a seat," he said. Madison quickly sat down. "Now turn your legs, place one hand in your lap and hold the other one outstretched like Elizabeth in the painting." She did as instructed and froze in her place.

Spencer paused as he studied first the painting, then Madison. His eyes darted quickly from one to the other and back again.

"Hurry up," said Madison. "My arm is getting..."

"That's it!" Spencer shouted. "I found it!"

"What did you find?" she asked.

"Remember when I told you to look for what is not there? What I should have said is to look at the painting for what is there and is really not there."

Madison walked over to the portrait. "What are you talking about?"

"In the portrait, she seems to be pointing at something. What is she pointing at?"

Madison studied the painting. "I don't get it."

"The doorway," said Spencer. "She's pointing at a doorway in the painting, and there is no doorway."

"Someone has sealed up the door? Why would they do that?"

"It means that there is a hidden room somewhere behind that wall," said Spencer. "And if ever there was a more perfect place to hide the jewelry, this is it."

"How do we get in?" she asked.

"You still don't get it, do you? This is where we hang the tapestry with the rose. Unless I miss my guess, the key will slip though the slit and into a lock. Even the hooks for hanging the tapestry are still in the wall."

"Well, let's do it," she said.

Spencer pulled a chair to the wall and stepped onto it. "Hand me the tapestry," he said. Madison grabbed the tapestry from the floor and handed it to him. He slipped each corner over a hook in the wall and straightened the folds as best he could to allow it to flatten out against the wall. Spencer then stepped off the chair and pulled it out of the way.

Excitedly, he fished in his pocket for the key and held it in his outstretched hand. "Would you like to do the honors?" he asked.

Madison smiled. "I think the honor belongs to you," she said.

With one hand, Spencer gently pulled on the tapestry to straighten it out. With his other hand, he inserted the key through the tiny opening and forced it through the wallpaper. It hit metal. Spencer slid the key over the surface until it fell into an opening. He turned the key and felt a bolt unlatch.

"We're almost there," he said. He pulled on the key, and the door opened.

"Look at that," said Madison. "The outline of the door is hidden in the designs of the wallpaper."

Spencer pulled the tapestry to the floor and opened the door. It was dark inside. He fumbled for a switch on the wall and snapped it on. A single overhead light fixture came to life bathing the room in a soft dim light. It was a small room with a single bed in the middle. There was a small nightstand next to it with several books piled on top. On the other side of the bed was a wheel chair backed up against the wall.

"Something tells me this was a secret room," said Spencer.

"Why do you say that?" asked Madison.

"Not only was the door purposely hidden, but the windows have been sealed shut. Somebody was hiding out in here, and from the looks of that wheel chair, they had a medical condition as well."

Madison slowly crossed the room. "Who do you suppose it was?"

"I don't know, but I get the feeling they were in here for a long time, and whoever lived here died in that bed."

"How can you tell that?" she asked.

"The wheel chair," said Spencer. "It's backed up against that wall. The last time the person living in here left this room, they were carried out."

Madison's eyes darted from the wheel chair to the door. "It was my great grandmother, wasn't it?"

"I don't know."

"What would be your guess?"

"I just don't have enough information. Do we even know whatever became of Elizabeth?"

"No, but I'll bet the letters will tell us something," she said.

Spencer walked slowly across the room. "By the way, I think we've forgotten why we broke into this room in the first place."

"You and those jewels," said Madison. "Is that all you ever think about?"

"Spoken like a truly rich person," said Spencer.

"This isn't about money."

Spencer smiled. "Oh, so, when I find the treasure, you don't want any of it?"

"I didn't say that."

Spencer stopped in one corner of the room. On a small table was a chessboard with a small cross sitting on one of the squares. He picked up the piece. "I'll bet this is another clue."

"What is that in your hand?" she asked.

"I don't know," he said. "It's some kind of a small cross with R.I.P. carved on the front of it."

Madison raced across the room and took the small wooden piece from Spencer. "I know what this is. This represents a cemetery stone and wherever it was on the chessboard, is the location of the grave in the cemetery."

"How did you know that?" asked Spencer.

"I was on a scavenger hunt when I was a kid, and this was one of the clues for finding a treasure."

Spencer glanced at the chessboard. "Then this board is the cemetery?"

"On which square was the cross sitting?"

Spencer set it back down. "Right here," he said. He pointed at an X that was carved into the wood on the other side of the board. "Wonder what that means?"

"In chess, that's the spot for a pawn. My guess, the jewelry is buried where the cross was, which is the location for the queen."

"What do you think it all means?"

"I know how this must sound, but I think you'll find the jewelry in the grave at that location," said Madison.

"And if you're wrong, who are we digging up?"

"We won't know that until we see the tombstone."

A smile spread slowly across Spencer's face. "Then let's go."

# CHAPTER EIGHTEEN

It was early evening when Spencer and Madison pulled into the cemetery. The setting sun spread shadowy fingers, giving the landscape an eerie, almost unworldly appearance. Spencer stopped the car just inside the entrance.

"Maybe this isn't such a good idea," he said, his voice weak and quivering.

"You're scared of ghosts, aren't you?" asked Madison.

"No, I'm not scared of them," he said. "I just think they don't mind visitors during the day. After dark, the place belongs to them, and visitors suddenly become intruders."

"You really are some kind of tough guy, aren't you?"

"I just believe that cemeteries are closed after dark for a reason."

Madison pointed at the road ahead. "Just drive to the back of the cemetery, and don't worry. I'll protect you."

Spencer eased the car in gear and slowly drove down the single lane dirt road. At the rear of the cemetery, the road intersected with another dirt road. Spencer stopped the car and turned off the engine. By then, the sun had all but set, and the dark gray sky was giving way to inky black.

"Well, I've seen enough," said Spencer.

Madison opened the car door. "Grab the chessboard, and let's go."

They both got out of the car and started for the last row of tombstones.

"How many tombstones over from the end are we?" she asked. She pulled a small flashlight from her purse and pointed it at the chessboard.

Spencer counted the squares on the chessboard then the tombstones. He pointed at a tall monument in the shape of a cross. "That should be the one," he said.

They hurried across the grounds and stopped in front of the dark gray granite marker.

"The grave is not that old," said Spencer.

"That's because she died two years ago," said Madison.

"Who is it? I can't see the inscription."

"Elizabeth Longberry," she said. "I think we hit pay dirt."

Spencer smiled. "I have a good feeling about this."

"Just one problem."

"What's that?"

"My guess is the jewelry is buried with her. How bad do you want it?"

"She wouldn't do that."

"I know you fell in love with her, but I really don't think you want to see her after two years of decomposing."

Spencer gazed at the tombstone. "And they say you can't take it with you."

"This isn't like her," said Madison. "I can't believe she would lead us to such a morbid discovery."

"I agree, but that doesn't tell us what's buried here."

"I say the jewelry is buried here," said Madison. "All this time and all these clues have been directing us to find the jewelry. She wouldn't have us jump through all these hoops and then lead us to a dead body."

"Well, for the really big question, if she's not buried here, where then is she buried?"

"There's only one other place to check," said Madison. She pointed at the chessboard. "Remember the X carved on it? Count the number of squares and tell me which tombstone it is."

Spencer counted over six and down five. "There it is," he said pointing at two small, unassuming, yet identical tombstones. The left side had mounded dirt and no grass. He dropped to his knees and brushed away leaves that were covering the face of the stone. "Unless I counted wrong, your theory didn't work out. The name on this tombstone is Elizabeth Browning."

"Elizabeth Browning," muttered Madison. "I wonder who that is."

Spencer leaned closer to the stone. "Well, maybe we don't know who Elizabeth Browning is, but there is a definite relationship to the other grave. This one died July 18, 1995, that's the same date as the other."

Madison thought for a moment. "What's the name on the tombstone next to hers?"

Spencer leaned closer again. "Harrison Ellington," he announced. "This is the future resting spot for my great grandfather." He jumped to his feet. "I don't get it."

"I'm not sure why the name Browning is on that tombstone, but I'll tell you one thing I do know. My great grandmother is buried here. Where else would she want to be buried other than right next to the love of her life?"

"Then that proves the jewelry is buried over there at the cross," said Spencer. "I'll go get the shovel out of the car."

"You brought a shovel?"

"It's called planning ahead," he said.

Spencer grabbed the shovel from the trunk of his car and slowly walked over to the grave. Madison stood next to him.

"Well," she said.

"Well, what?" asked Spencer.

"What's the problem now?"

"What makes you think there's a problem?"

"Unless that shovel starts digging up that grave by itself, we've got a problem," she said.

"Huh?"

"Why aren't you digging?"

"I'm catching my breath."

"From what?"

"I don't know. Getting the shovel."

"You're scared to death, aren't you?"

"Well, what if you're wrong about this whole thing? What if she is buried here?" said Spencer.

"We've already been over this," she said. "She's not buried here."

"What if someone sees us digging up a grave? Aren't there laws about such stuff?"

Madison pointed at the ground. "Dig!"

Nearly a half-hour passed before Spencer finally hit a metal object with his shovel. He carefully dug around the box and pulled it out of the open grave. It was an old box in good condition. It was hinged with a hasp and no padlock.

"I'll let you do the honors," said Spencer. He took the flashlight from her and pointed it at the box.

Madison knelt down and gently lifted the hasp. She grasped both sides of the lid and slowly opened it.

"Dear God!" said Madison.

"And then some," said Spencer.

Inside were layers of bracelets, necklaces, rings, and earrings, all matching and all diamond-studded. Madison picked up a bracelet and held it in the light. "That's the most beautiful thing I've ever seen," she said, her voice raspy with excitement.

"We're rich," said Spencer.

Two shadowy figures stepped forward. "No, you're not," said Frank Luigi. "But we are."

Spencer spun around and pointed the flashlight at the two men. Frank was pointing a gun in his direction.

"Who are you?" asked Spencer.

"The name is Frank Luigi, and this is my brother, Melvin. I tell you that because I think you deserve to know the name of the men who are not only going to take you for a boat ride, but are going to relieve you of the contents of that box."

"How do you know what is in this box?" asked Spencer.

"We've been on to you for quite some time," said Frank. "We just thought we'd let you do all the work finding the jewelry."

"How thoughtful," muttered Spencer.

Frank motioned with his gun. "Now get moving, the two of you. We have a boat to catch."

+++

It was nearly midnight when Frank's car stopped at a dock at the water's edge. Spencer and Madison were forced out of the car and stood in front of a rusted freighter that loomed into the night sky. The wind howled as a storm rolled in from the west, causing the giant ship to pitch and toss in the water.

Frank gave Spencer a gentle shove. "Get up that gangplank," he said. In spite of the swaying and jerking of the small wooden gangplank, Spencer led Madison to the rain-soaked deck. Frank and Melvin then led them across the deck to a small door at the wheelhouse. Frank knocked on the door and it swung open to allow them access.

"Well, we finally meet," said Charlie Stenger, holding the door open. "I've been waiting for this moment."

"Who are you?" asked Spencer, still holding the box of jewelry.

"My name is Charlie Stenger. That name may not mean much to you now, but in the short time you have to live, it will become most significant."

"What do you want with us?" asked Madison.

"It's not what I want with you, but rather what I want from you. In fact, while we're on the subject, hand over the box."

Spencer didn't move. Frank cocked the hammer of his gun and held it to Spencer's head. He still held onto the box.

"Do you really want to give up your life for a box of gems?" asked Charlie.

"You're going to kill us anyhow," said Spencer.

"Perhaps," said Charlie. "But at least it's only a possibility and somewhere down the road. This is a certainty and it's right now."

Spencer paused as he considered the options and then slowly handed over the treasure. "How did you know about the jewelry?"

"I work for the insurance company that paid off the claim made on this jewelry nearly a hundred years ago."

"And I suppose you're going to turn it into the insurance company," said Spencer.

Charlie snickered. "Yeah, you keep believing that and the tooth fairy as well."

"Doesn't seem fair," said Spencer. "We worked hard for those jewels."

"That you did," said Charlie. "I would have given up a long time ago. The boys and I got tired just watching you."

"So, what happens to us?" Spencer asked.

"Frank, show our guests to their new accommodations," said Charlie.

Frank opened the door and motioned with his gun for them to leave. "By the way, Charlie, are we going to be all right with this storm coming up?"

Charlie patted the massive steering wheel in front of him. "We're getting under way in just a few minutes, and you have nothing to worry about. This old tub can take winds over a hundred miles per hour."

"Wish you wouldn't call her an old tub," muttered Frank, as he closed the door.

Outside on the deck, the wind had escalated to gale strength. Huge waves broke over the sides of the ship washing anything not nailed down over the side. Frank led them to a door about midship. Inside was a ladder that took them to the lower level. He then led them to another door that opened into an empty hold.

"Tie their hands and feet," said Frank to Melvin. "We want them to feel right at home."

Melvin motioned for both Madison and Spencer to sit on the floor. By that time, water was nearly six inches deep and rising. The bilge pumps were not keeping up with the water splashing into the boat. Melvin neatly tied their hands and feet and backed them against a wall.

"You can't leave us down here," said Spencer. "We'll drown."

"Imagine that," said Frank. "Bet you never guessed you'd end your life in a hell hole like this."

"I'll give you a million dollars if you let us go," said Madison.

"You know, that's very generous of you, but money isn't really the issue right now," said Frank. "Charlie has promised to cut us in when we sell the jewelry."

"And you believe that he can sell the jewelry?" asked Spencer. "Nobody is going to touch the stuff. You know it, and I know it. The stuff will be much too hot."

Frank started for the door. "Sorry, but I trust Charlie. If he says he'll take care of us, that's what he will do."

"Oh, yeah," said Spencer. "Honor among thieves, and all that. If you had any honor at all, you would at least save Madison here. She's a woman, for God's sake, and you can't kill a woman like this."

Frank opened the door, and Melvin stepped up and grabbed it. "He's right, you know," said Melvin. "You ain't suppose to kill women. They don't even do it in the movies."

Frank pushed the door open against Melvin's will. "Who said anything about killing her or the guy, for that matter? They're just taking a boat ride, and they should have bought first class tickets."

Frank left the room while Melvin stared at the two helpless beings.

"Help us, Melvin," said Spencer. "You know they aren't going to let us go. I can see you want to do the right thing, and the right thing is to let us go." Melvin didn't move. "At least spare the lady, Melvin. You know that's the right thing to do."

Melvin paused for a moment and then started for Madison when Frank shouted, "Come on, Melvin. We've got work to do."

Suddenly, he turned and walked out of the room. Frank slammed the door shut behind his brother and locked it with a sliding metal bar.

"As if things weren't bad enough, they had to lock the door as well," said Spencer.

"It seemed like you were making progress with Melvin," said Madison. "He looked like he was going to help, right up until Frank jumped in."

"I think we were getting through to him," said Spencer.

Madison smiled. "And whoever said chivalry was dead? I was impressed with your plea to spare me."

Spencer blushed. "Any man would have done the same thing."

"No, they wouldn't," she said." I don't know of another man who would have done that."

From deep in the bowels of the ship, a motor came to life. The ship shuddered and groaned as it pulled away from the dock.

"We must be getting under way," said Spencer.

"Wonder where we're going," she said. "It can't be good for us."

The ship lurched from side to side.

"I just hope this old tub can take it," said Spencer.

The engine grew louder as the ship sped into open water.

"Well, what do we do now?" she asked.

"I don't know. I guess we wait to see where they're taking us."

"Spence, I've been wondering about something."

Spencer smiled. "This can't be good."

"I know we've only been together for a short time, but in that short time we've found some of the most valuable jewelry in the world, we've pieced together a romance that happened some eighty years ago, and we even made love. Now, I don't mind telling you that I don't make love with just any Tom, Dick, or Harry. I even told you that I love you while we were doing it, but through it all, I don't think I ever heard you express your feelings one way or the other about me."

Spencer forced a smile. He looked away. "I know I haven't been what you would call a romantic person. It's not that I don't have feelings for you. I do. In fact, I …I"

"You're having trouble even saying the word."

"I know, it's just that I've always been such a loser with women. I've always said the wrong things. I'm surprised my wife stayed with me as long as she did."

"Well, here's your chance," she said. "How do you feel about me? I think I have a right to know."

Spencer glanced around the room. "You want to know right now? I have a feeling these guys plan to finish us off, and you want to know how I feel about you?"

"Actually, I can't think of a better time."

Spencer took a deep breath and began to stammer. "I think you're the most beautiful woman I've ever met. You're charming, fun to be with, and you like to watch scary movies."

"Scary movies? What do they have to do with anything?"

"I figure everybody likes scary movies, and anybody who says they don't is not being honest."

Madison paused and smiled. "I thought you said you were lousy with women."

"I am."

"What you just told me was one of the sweetest things any man ever said to me," she said.

"I love you, Madison," he said. "I love you very much, and if we ever get out of this mess…"

Just then, the ship was hit by a huge wave. It rolled sending them sprawling across the floor. Water gushed into the room drenching Spencer and Madison. Just as the ship seemed as if it were about to roll completely over, it righted itself with a sudden jerk.

"That was close," said Spencer.

"You were about to say something."

"No, I wasn't."

"Yes, you were. You started to say something about if we ever get out of this mess."

"Oh, yeah. I was about to say that if we ever get out of this mess, I'd like to ask you to marry me."

"You hardly know me," she said.

"Is that important?"

"It is to me," she said. "But I'll consider your offer."

"I didn't make an offer."

"Oh, yeah. Well, if you do…"

A silence fell in the room. Finally, Spencer decided to change the subject.

"What was it like being married to one of the richest men in America?" he asked.

"I can best answer that question with a question," said Madison. "How would you feel if the one you love sent you a Valentine's card signed by a secretary? Or opened presents from your spouse and he's just as surprised as you, since he didn't pick it out or wrap in the first place?"

"Other than that, was he a good husband?"

"I don't know," said Madison. "I never saw him. He worked all the time. I literally had to make appointments with my own husband."

Another rogue wave slammed into the side of the ship. It lurched to starboard so hard it nearly rolled over. The ship shuddered and groaned as it struggled to right itself once more, this time listing to starboard and sitting low in the water. Madison and Spencer skidded across the floor slamming into the wall. Water poured down the hallways and into all the rooms.

Spencer stared at the water as it rapidly spread across the floor. "I don't know much about boats, but I'd say this one is in trouble."

"Maybe we should try getting out of here," said Madison.

"Scoot over here, and we'll put our backs together," said Spencer. "Maybe I can untie your hands."

They positioned themselves with their backs to each other. Spencer wiggled his hands until they were free enough to grab her ropes.

"I don't know what kind of knot he tied, but I can tell you he's no seaman," he said.

Madison leaned back to get her tied hands closer to Spencer. "What will we do then? The door is locked."

"I don't know," said Spencer. "Let's take it one step at a time."

He fumbled with the ropes until he finally freed one end. He slipped it through, over and under, until they went limp and dropped to the floor. Madison leaned over and untied her feet, then turned to untie Spencer.

"Damn! Feels good to be free," said Spencer jumping to his feet.

"Now what?" said Madison, slowly getting up.

"Follow me," he said. "I've got an idea."

He walked to the back of the hold where a pile of boxes was stacked against a large metal file cabinet. He nudged the cabinet with his shoulder until it moved out of the way revealing an unlocked steel door. He turned the handle and it swung open leading them to another empty hold.

They were halfway across the room when another rogue wave slammed into the ship. With the added weight of the extra water that had flooded the lower levels, she rolled over, her once proud mast easing precariously into the water. Large volumes of water flooded into the dying ship, racing down hallways and seeking out every corner of the ship.

Their small world turned upside down, Spencer took hold of Madison and helped her through a door that led to a hallway that was already waist deep in water. They trudged through the heavy water, half-swimming and half-wading. They turned a corner that led to a locked door.

"What do we do now?" asked Madison.

Spencer pointed down another corridor. "There's a ladder at the other end," he shouted.

By that time, the water had flooded nearly every compartment of the ship. The bow slowly dropped below the surface of the murky water lifting the stern high into the air. Huge waves slammed relentlessly into the crippled beast ensuring her inevitable death.

With one arm around Madison, Spencer swam through the cold swirling water until he latched onto a rung of the ladder. He helped her gain her footing and guided her up the steps. The water swirled and eddied, consuming everything in its path. Madison reached the top of the ladder and squeezed through the opening that led to the upper deck. The water was rapidly flooding the lower deck and by then was within two feet of the ceiling.

His head already under water, Spencer started up the ladder. Just as he reached the top, and filled his lungs with air, the ship violently lurched to starboard causing the hinged iron grate to slam shut on the opening. With both hands, Spencer pushed the grate. It didn't budge. He shook it. Nothing. The water swirled upwards until it was at his neck.

"Madison, get me out of here!" he shouted.

She bent over and tugged at the grate while he pushed from below. Still nothing.

"It's stuck," she said.

"Find something to pry it open," said Spencer.

Madison glanced one way then the other. "There isn't anything! What should I do?"

By then, the water was within inches of the ceiling. Spencer turned his head sideways to flatten it against the bottom of the grate. "Try pulling on the grate again!"

Madison dropped to one knee. She heard Spencer gasp for air as the water swirled over his head and up through the grate. She looked down through the water-covered grate. She could see him staring at her through the murky water.

"Dear God, please let this be another bad dream!" she said. She grabbed the grate with both hands and shook it. "I don't want to lose him again!"

Outside, the storm raged violently. The ship was still lying on its side and was nearly submerged. Waves pounded against her as if to drive it into its watery grave.

Then suddenly, the ship was pushed into a whirlpool that spun it completely around. At the same time, from out of nowhere, a rogue wave nearly two stories high came at the foundering ship. The swells from the approaching monster lifted the mast and hull of the ship straight up in the water setting it down like a toy boat in a bathtub. Water poured from every port and deck. It bobbed and wavered, nearly falling again into its grave, but instead it steadied itself as if wanting a second chance.

Down in the bowels of the ship, two people scrambled to save themselves. As the rogue wave hit, the violent force that slammed the ship nearly lifting her out of the water, threw Madison against a wall. As the ship turned, the huge mass of water below deck pounded the grate, springing it free. Spencer shot through the opening and broke to the surface of the water. His lungs nearly exploded as he sucked in the moisture-laden stale air.

"Are you all right?" shouted Madison above the roar of the water.

"Yeah. How 'bout you?"

"I'm okay."

"Then let's get out of here!" he said.

Up on deck, the night sky was ink black. Mountainous, gray clouds glided silently in and out of the dark sky giving it an eerie, ghost-like appearance. Spencer walked over to the side of the ship and through the dim moonlight could see that the storm had abated. With unceasing determination, the waves continued to crash into the hull of the ship, but with little effect.

"The storm seems to have died down," said Spencer.

"I wonder where that Charlie guy and his friends are," said Madison.

Spencer's eyes caught the movement of an object on the other side of the ship. It seemed to move in time with the swaying ship. "I think I found one of them," he said and started cautiously across the deck. He stopped in front of the dark shadowy figure of a lifeless man seemingly pinned to the side of the ship. He bent down to examine the body.

"It's Charlie, all right," said Spencer. "He must have somehow caught his belt on this post when the ship capsized."

"Is he dead?" asked Madison.

"As a doornail," Spencer replied.

"Wonder where his friends are."

Spencer quickly glanced around the deck. "My guess is they weren't even as lucky as Charlie here."

Madison jumped. "The jewelry!"

Without saying another word, Spencer bolted for the wheelhouse. He opened the door and stepped inside. It was dark. Only a sliver of moonlight penetrated the interior through a window. Water still slowly dripped from the ceiling and the walls. Spencer walked slowly across the room in search of the small metal chest. He was nearly to the other side when he stumbled over something. He reached down and picked up a small box.

Before he could open it, he heard a scream from outside the wheelhouse. "Spencer, come here!" shouted Madison.

He tucked the box under his arm and bolted out the door. "What's wrong?" he asked.

She pointed at the horizon. "Look what's coming!"

Coming at them from the east was a multitude of lights from Coast Guard rescue ships and aircraft. Above the din, was the unmistakable whap-whap sound of a helicopter as it glided over the waves, in advance of the others. It stopped and hovered overhead as one of the smaller and faster surface ships raced to the scene.

Spencer set the box down and wrapped his arms around Madison. "I love you," he said with a smile and kissed her long and hard.

"I love you, too," she said.

The ride back in the small boat was long and bumpy. By the time they reached land, Spencer had twice leaned over the side. Once out of the boat, they were escorted to a waiting limousine parked nearby. A man dressed in a dark suit opened the rear passenger door.

Spencer hesitated. "Where are we going?"

"I assure you that you are in safe hands," he said. "I was sent here to pick you up by Mr. Bradley McKinley."

"Uncle Bradley!" blurted Madison.

Spencer bent over and peeked inside. "Where is he?"

"Mr. McKinley is back home. He was released from the hospital today."

They slid across the seat and closed the door. The driver got behind the wheel.

"By the way," said Spencer. "How did Mr. McKinley know where we were?"

The driver started the engine and glanced in the rearview mirror. "I'm afraid you'll have to ask Mr. McKinley that question. I'm not at liberty to answer that."

Spencer smiled and nonchalantly waved his hand. "Then let's go."

# CHAPTER NINETEEN

Bradley was leaning back, asleep in his easy chair when Spencer and Madison came through the front door. The opening of the door aroused him from his sleep.

"Uncle Bradley, you're home," said Madison.

He leaned forward snapping the chair upright. "Hi, kids," he said, his voice groggy from sleep. "Glad to see you made it back home."

"How are you feeling?" asked Madison.

"I'm fine, just a little tired," he said, his voice frail and raspy.

"Are you home for good, or do you have to go back?" she asked.

"They said I'm fit as a fiddle," he said. "They just didn't finish the statement by saying for a man of his age."

"Mr. McKinley, may I ask you a question?" said Spencer.

"Yes, you may," said Bradley. "But call me Bradley. The only Mr. McKinley I ever knew was my father, and he's long gone."

"I just wanted to know how you knew where we were?"

"I've been keeping an eye on you two for quite sometime," Bradley said. "Or, at least, I've had someone keeping an eye on you two." He nodded at the chest under Spencer's arm. "I see you found it."

Spencer carefully set the treasure in Bradley's lap. He turned the hasp and swung open the lid. Bradley leaned over and smiled. He gently picked up a bracelet and held it to the light. "It's more beautiful than I remembered."

Spencer took a seat on the couch, Madison sitting next to him. "Somehow, I get the feeling you've known more about this than you're telling," said Spencer, smiling coyly. "Elizabeth didn't hide the clues. It was you, wasn't it?"

Bradley tenderly shifted his weight in the chair. "They were all her idea. She thought of every clue," he said. "She just wasn't capable of carrying them out. Actually, I had a great deal of fun. The horseshoe thing on the tombstone...that was my idea."

"But why?" asked Spencer. "Why make us jump through all those hoops?"

The old man smiled and settled back in his chair. "Before I answer that question, let me ask you one. How are you two getting along?"

Spencer quickly glanced at Madison. "I'm in love with her."

Madison looked away with a shyness she had never felt. "When you consider the shaky start we had, we've come a long way."

"So you love him," said Bradley.

"I didn't say that!" she blurted. She paused. "Well, maybe a little bit."

"Then she accomplished what she wanted to do," he said. "She knew that a common goal would bind any relationship."

"But how did she know it would be someone like us?" asked Madison.

"That was the real mystery of your great grandmother," said Bradley. "She was quite a woman. There were many things about her I just couldn't explain. I'm not so sure she hasn't had something to do with what's happening today."

Spencer leaned forward, his interest piqued. "What do you mean?" he asked.

"I know it sounds crazy, but I have felt her presence."

"You mean you think her spirit is here with us?" asked Spencer.

"I feel it every day."

"Maybe you just miss her and confuse that emotion with a sense that she is here."

"I've lost many close people in my life, people who were as close to me as she was, but I never had this feeling. Her spirit is restless because there are things undone, things she needs to put to rest."

"What are those things?" asked Madison.

"I promise I'll explain everything in due time, my child, but first there is something very important I need from the two of you."

"What is it?" she asked.

"I want you to take me to see Harrison," said Bradley.

Spencer glanced at Madison. His face had a look of desperation. "We'd be happy to, but he sometimes is not in his right mind."

"Don't worry about that," said Bradley. "She won't let this important moment get away."

"Elizabeth?" asked Spencer.

Bradley struggled to get to his feet. "Right now, I need some sleep." He stopped and turned to Madison. "Can I count on you to take me to see him?"

"I'll make all the arrangements," she said.

He lightly patted her on the shoulder. "Good night to both of you."

+ + +

It was nearly eight in the morning when Bradley trudged down the stairs and into the kitchen. Madison was standing near the stove, and Spencer was setting the table.

"Morning, kids," said Bradley.

"Good morning, Uncle Bradley," said Madison. "I was just coming to get you. I have hot pancakes coming off the griddle."

Bradley walked over to the table and set down two large scrapbooks. "Sleep well, Spencer?" he asked, taking a seat at the table.

"Very well, thank you," said Spencer.

Madison set a plate of sizzling sausage and another piled high with pancakes on the table, and they all took a seat.

Bradley dropped a pancake on his plate and smothered it with syrup. "Nearly ninety years old, and I still can't get enough of the sweets."

Madison took the bottle and turned it upside down. "It must run in the family. Pancakes are like cake. I eat the pancakes for the syrup, just like I eat cake for the icing."

Bradley took a bite and then sipped his coffee. "I know it's early, but do you think we can leave to see Harrison today?"

"Everything is all set," said Madison. "We have a flight out this afternoon."

"That's excellent," he said. "Just excellent."

Spencer took a bit of his breakfast and then set down his fork. "Bradley, I don't mean to pry, but you mentioned last night that you have something to tell us."

"Oh, I have much to tell you," he said with a smile. "But I'm afraid you'll have to wait for me to finish these delicious pancakes." He turned to Madison. "You always were a good cook, now that I think about it."

"Thanks, Uncle Bradley," she said.

"Tell me something," said Bradley. "What have you decided to do with the jewelry?"

Madison and Spencer exchanged glances. "I guess we never gave it much thought," she said.

"Might I suggest that you get it locked up until you do decide," he said. "There are people out there who would do unspeakable things for a lot less."

"Uncle Bradley, that brings up a question of utmost importance," she said. "She boarded the Titanic in third class, and yet she had in her possession some of the most valuable jewelry in the world. It left us no choice, but to believe that she was a thief."

Bradley leaned back and laughed aloud. He set down his fork and wiped his mouth with a napkin. "I can see how you would make that mistake. She did her best to pose as third class, but I hardly think she fooled many of the other passengers."

"Then she wasn't a thief?" asked Spencer.

"Well, there are those who would say she was stealing the jewelry, even though it belonged to her. There was a man back in England who certainly felt that way."

"Uncle Bradley, you're not making much sense."

"Your great grandmother's real name was Elizabeth Browning," he said.

"Elizabeth Browning…that name sounds familiar," said Madison.

"We saw it on a tombstone in the cemetery," said Spencer.

"That's where she was laid to rest," said Bradley.

"Why so many names?" asked Spencer.

"In England, your great grandmother was royalty. In fact, she was the Duchess of Devonshire. She lived in a castle of sorts, had servants, and whatever else goes with the title."

"Wow," said Spencer. "I'm consorting with royalty."

"That's what I thought," said Bradley. "However, she said it was a title only, not much power to the position. Anyhow, it was about two years into the marriage that Elizabeth realized she had made a mistake. Actually, from what she told me, he showed his true colors within the first month. I guess she just figured he would change, and he did. He began to abuse her physically. You know, I always figured there's a special place in hell for guys who beat their wives."

"Let me guess," said Spencer. "She left him with the jewelry and came to America on the Titanic. Why the Titanic?"

"I remember her saying she knew there would be large crowds, and that it would be easier to hide, in case he followed her or had her followed."

"Did he follow her?" Madison asked.

"Oh, yes, indeed. For a good many years as well."

Spencer finished eating and leaned back from the table. "So when the Titanic went down, so did her identity."

"Depends on whose identity you're talking about," said Bradley. "Elizabeth Browning simply disappeared, while Elizabeth York died on the Titanic. For some reason, she kept the York name, even though Elizabeth York died on the Titanic. I guess she figured America was a big place, and there certainly must be more than one Elizabeth York."

"I knew her as Longberry," said Madison. "When did she change her name to that?"

"That came years later when she got married," said Bradley.

"She got married!" shouted Madison. "I thought she was in love with Spencer's great grandfather."

"She was in love with Harrison," said Bradley. "In fact, she loved him all the rest of her life."

"I guess I don't understand," said Spencer. "She was in love with Grandpa Harrison, and yet she married someone by the name of Longberry?"

Bradley smiled. "The rest of that puzzle will be solved when we talk with your great grandfather."

"Speaking of puzzles," said Spencer. "I sense that Elizabeth was no ordinary woman. I have these extraordinary dreams, and I get messages through old photographs. No one can convince me that they aren't from her."

Bradley picked up the scrapbooks and handed one to Madison and one to Spencer. They thumbed through the pages. They were filled with photographs taken throughout their lives.

"I don't get it," said Spencer. "Here's a picture taken of me at my tenth birthday party. I remember it very well, because it was the only birthday I was allowed to have friends over. But I don't remember this picture."

"Here's a picture of me at my graduation," said Madison. "I don't remember this photo."

"There must be a hundred photos of me in this scrapbook, and I've never seen a one," said Spencer. "Who took them?"

"I did," Bradley announced.

"Why, Uncle Bradley?" asked Madison.

"Your great grandmother chose you and Spencer. She chose you before either of you were born."

"Chose us for what?" asked Madison.

Bradley picked up another book. This one was much smaller, bound in black leather and worn from much use.

"I can best answer that question by reading from her personal diary," said Bradley. He leafed through the pages, then stopped midway through. "She wrote this in 1954, long before either of you was born. 'In years to come, they will be born and grow to young adults. Their first meeting will result in disdain for one another. They will be an unlikely match, these two, but their feelings for each other will flourish in spite of themselves. It is their destiny to fulfill that, which was beyond my reach. They will succeed where I failed. They will mend the broken circle and end the pain I have suffered all these years.'"

Bradley's voice quivered. He closed the book and wiped his eyes with the back of his hand. "When you two were born, she knew. Even back then. She wanted to know everything about you, how you did in school, who your friends were, everything. And that's where I came in. Unbeknownst to you, I became a part of your lives. I made the scrapbooks that you have in front of you. I only hope you are not offended by such an invasion of privacy."

Madison held out her hand. "May I see the diary?"

"Certainly," he said and handed it to her.

She began leafing through the pages.

Spencer's face was blank. He glanced at the scrapbook and then turned to Bradley. "How could she have known I would be the one?"

"That's just it," he said. "I don't know."

"I mean I could see her choosing Madison," said Spencer. "She's from her own family, but how could she pick someone she didn't even know?"

Bradley pointed at the scrapbook in front of Spencer. "Turn to the first page. In that photo, you're not even one year old. That was the first snapshot I took of you."

"She knew when I was born that I was the one," said Spencer, nearly muttering to himself.

"Well, I have to ask the question," said Spencer. "What is it that we are supposed to do? It's obvious we were chosen, but for what?"

"In due time," said Bradley with a smile.

Madison looked up from reading the diary. "Uncle Bradley, the handwriting changes on this page. It's almost like there were two different people writing in it."

"That's my handwriting," said Bradley. "I took over after her accident."

"Accident? What accident?" asked Spencer. "You didn't tell us about any accident."

"There are many things I have to discuss with your great grandfather before I talk about these things," said Bradley. "I hope you don't mind, but I think you will understand later."

"When was the last time you saw my great grandfather?" asked Spencer.

"He went off to the war in 1914, and that was the last time I talked with him," said Spencer. "I've seen him a few times over the years, but haven't talked to him."

"Do you think he will remember you?" asked Spencer.

Bradley smiled. "Yes, he will remember me."

"How can you be so sure?"

"There are only a few things in this life that are a certainty, and this is one of them," said Bradley.

Spencer got up from the table and took his empty plate to the sink. "I just hope his mind is okay when we get there. It comes and goes."

Bradley smiled. "His mind will be just fine."

"How can you be so sure of that?" said Spencer. "He's delirious more times than not."

"Elizabeth will not let it happen," he said. "I have something to give to your grandfather from her."

Madison moved her chair next to Bradley. "Uncle Bradley, you have to tell us what that is. I think you will agree we have more than just a passing interest in this thing."

"I'm sorry, child," he said. "But I simply cannot discuss this before I have a chance to talk with Harrison. I will allow you both to remain in the room while we talk. I think you both have earned that, but I must insist that you both stay quiet while I talk with him. This is a very important meeting."

"Well, I can promise you I'll be quiet," said Spencer, then turned to Madison with a grin. "But I can't make any promises for your granddaughter."

Bradley smiled and got to his feet. "I guess I should go pack for the trip."

"We'll be leaving in just a couple hours," said Spencer.

"Sounds great," said Bradley as he left the room.

 # Chapter Twenty

The next morning brought gray, overcast skies. Dark, ominous clouds hung like a shroud over the city of Detroit. Spencer and Madison were having breakfast in the hotel restaurant when Bradley joined them.

"Good morning, kids," he said, taking a seat at the table.

"Good morning, Uncle Bradley," said Madison, sliding her empty plate out of his way.

Spencer picked up a carafe and held it over a cup next to Bradley. "Care for a cup of coffee?" he asked.

Bradley opened his napkin, then put it back down. "Sounds great. Have you two already eaten?"

"Yes, we did, Uncle Bradley," said Madison. "We didn't expect you until later, but go ahead and order. We're in no hurry."

"Oh, I'm not hungry," he said. "The coffee will be fine."

Spencer sipped his coffee. "Bradley, if you don't mind my asking, did you get any sleep last night? You seem a bit edgy."

Bradley's hand shook as he picked up his coffee and drank it. "Didn't sleep a wink."

"Was your bed uncomfortable?" asked Madison.

"No, nothing like that," he replied. "I guess I'm just nervous about meeting Harrison."

"You seemed so confident yesterday," said Spencer. "What happened?"

"I don't know. I guess I finally realized just how important this meeting is, not just for me, but for Harrison and Elizabeth as well."

"I thought you said Elizabeth died," said Spencer.

"She did."

"Then why did you mention that this will be for her as well?"

"Oh, she'll be there," said Bradley. "You can bet on that. She wouldn't miss this for anything."

Bradley began to fumble with a fork on the table until it fell on the floor. Spencer bent over and picked it up.

"Uncle Bradley, you mentioned once that you took care of my great grandmother for a lot of years," said Madison.

"Forty, to be exact."

"Was she an invalid?"

"She was confined to a wheelchair after the accident."

"I remember visiting you on several occasions and don't remember ever seeing her."

"After the accident, she unfortunately, did not want anyone to know she was alive. Remember the secret room that you found? That's where she spent the remainder of her life."

"Uncle Bradley, how could you keep her locked up in that little room?" asked Madison.

Bradley looked away. He looked troubled. "I begged her not to do it. I begged her year after year, even though deep down I knew she was right. It just didn't seem fair to waste her life. She was a beautiful woman even up until her death.

But the real beauty was on the inside. She was a real lady in every way. God, I miss her."

"Uncle Bradley, pardon me for prying, but you took care of her for over forty years," said Madison. "What kind of life was that for you?"

"Oh, I was right where I wanted to be," he said. "Technically, she wasn't really my mother, and she never did adopt me, but I loved her more than any man could love his own mother."

"I hate to say it," said Spencer. "But it almost seems like you were the one who wasted his life."

"I suppose it does to an outsider," said Bradley. "But God couldn't have been any kinder than to allow me to spend my life with that wonderful woman."

"Uncle Bradley, if you don't mind my saying, since you've been talking you seem to have relaxed a bit," said Madison.

Bradley breathed deeply and let it out. "Yes, I believe you're right." He jumped to his feet. "Let's go see Harrison Ellington."

It was a short trip to Oakwood Hospital taking less than fifteen minutes by cab. Bradley said nothing. His hands trembled as he got out of the car and crossed the parking lot. They checked in at the desk and took the elevator to the second floor. Room 211 was to the right and down the hall. It was quiet in the hallway, only an occasional nurse dashed in and out of rooms. Shoes clicking on the shiny tile floor echoed down the hall.

Bradley slowed his pace as he neared the room. Just outside 211, Bradley turned around and leaned against the wall. His hands were shaking violently, and he gasped for air.

"Are you okay?" asked Madison.

"Yes, child," he said. "I'll be okay. I just need to catch my breath."

"Do you want me to get you a chair?" asked Spencer.

"No, no. I'll be fine. Just give me a moment."

He didn't move for several minutes. His breathing was erratic, taking deep breaths one moment and short choppy ones another. In spite of the air conditioning, sweat beaded on his forehead.

After nearly five minutes, he stood straight, turned and took Madison's hand as he entered Room 211. As he passed through the doorway, Madison could feel his hand relax. She glanced at the old man beside her. His smile had returned and the sweat had disappeared from his forehead.

It was dark in the room. The only light came from a small lamp on the headboard. It smelled of antiseptic and dirty laundry. A nurse hovered over Harrison. She had just finished feeding him and was wiping his mouth with a rag. She seemed in a hurry as she scooped up her things in her arms.

"You members of the family?" she asked on her way to the door.

"Yes, we are," said Spencer.

"Well, even though it's against the rules, I'll close the door to give you privacy, and I'll be sure you're not disturbed."

"Thank you," said Spencer.

The three of them stood at the back of the room for a moment, not saying a word. The bright light from the lamp seemed to wash the features from his face. His ashen skin was white as snow, giving him an almost ghost-like appearance.

Suddenly, his eyes opened, and a smile appeared on his lips.

"She's here, you know," he said. "She's here in the room. We're all together once again. It's been so long."

"He's out of his head again," said Spencer.

Bradley took Spencer's hand and lightly patted it. "No, he's not," he said with a smile.

Spencer and Madison walked to the shadows of the foot of the bed while Bradley slowly walked over to Harrison.

"I knew you'd come," said Harrison. "She told me you would."

Bradley leaned over the bed, his face in the glow of the lamp. "Remember me?"

Harrison paused and then slowly turned his head in his direction. "You were just a tyke the last time I saw you, and I was a strapping young man." He chuckled. "Look at us now."

"Yes, my old friend," said Bradley. "Father Time has won again."

"Ha, Father Time beat the shit out of me, and he didn't do you any favors either."

They both smiled at one another as Harrison struggled to lift his head higher on the pillow.

"How's your health?" Bradley asked. "Do you think you'll be getting out of here in the near future?"

"Oh, I'll be getting out of here real soon, not the way you're thinking, but out of here just the same. They got one really nice-looking nurse here that I'd like to take with me, but I don't think she would want to go where I'm going."

"Is there anything I can get you?" asked Bradley.

The smile disappeared from Harrison's face. His sad eyes turned to Bradley as he strained to lift his head off the pillow. ""Give me peace," he said, his voice trembling. "I've been waiting for you. I know you're the one who will give me peace."

Bradley pulled a chair near the bed. He reached for Harrison's weathered hand and held it between his own.

"What happened, Harrison, all those years ago? I pieced together as much I could from the letters. I thought you had died when I read the letter from the War Department, then Elizabeth told me years later that you survived. It hurt her so much to talk about it, so I very seldom ever asked her any questions.

"Everyone thought I died, and, unfortunately, so did Elizabeth. I never did blame her. Why would she think anything else? The War Department declared me dead, killed in action. If you read that letter, you know how cold it sounds. I think someone should talk to them about their manners."

"She said something about you being held prisoner for over three years," said Bradley.

"Most God-awful experience of my life. No man should go through that, but that wasn't the worst thing that ever happened to me. No, sir. The worst came later when I came home to find that Elizabeth was married and had a baby. I don't think anybody can really know what pain is until they experience something like that. It wasn't her fault, you understand. She didn't know. She was as convinced as anybody that I was dead. I mean, after all, there were a lot of guys who didn't make it. The headlines were always full of the number of dead. It wasn't her fault. No, sir. She once said some time later that she had a gut feeling all along that I was still alive, but she met another guy and you know how that goes."

"Did you see her again?"

"I found out where she lived and sent her a letter. Didn't want to barge in on her and all seeing as how she had a family. Just didn't seem right. Besides, I wasn't sure how she would react, so I sent her a letter. She sent me one back and we agreed to meet in a restaurant. Never was quite sure why she picked a public place to meet after all that time. Guess she figured it was the right thing to do, being married and all. Didn't really matter much. That was the most thrilling thing that ever happened to me...still is."

"She didn't leave her husband, did she?"

"You know, I've loved that woman all my life. I've never stopped loving her to this day. Her beauty has haunted me to my very soul. But it was that very love for her that told me to walk away. She had a husband and a child. There was no room for me in her life."

"How did you know she wouldn't have gone with you? Did you ask her?" Bradley asked.

"It was too late for me. You see, I didn't want her looking over her shoulder. I guess I was a little jealous. I wanted her for myself."

"Years later, I married. I don't know why. It wasn't fair to her. She somehow knew there was someone else in my heart. I think she could see it in my eyes. Not the other woman, but the emptiness I felt inside. In time, her eyes grew cold as well, as the embers died. I've hated myself for what I did. It's bad enough I wasted my own life, but to ruin her life as well was unforgivable."

Bradley reached for a tissue and wiped the old man's eyes.

"You know, I've never told anyone about this," said Harrison. "I lived my life as a hermit, keeping to myself. Elizabeth has never approved, but I couldn't help myself. She was my first love and my only love. And just because she died doesn't change a thing. I can't stop loving her even after she's gone. I ask you, when a man loves a woman that much, is he supposed to stop loving her when she dies?"

Bradley paused for a moment and then slowly reached into his pocket. He pulled out a letter and held it in his hands.

"You know, Harrison, she never stopped loving you."

"Yes, but she married. She had to be in love with him."

"She thought she was in love, but when you met with her after coming back from the war, she knew she had to be with you. She tried to make a go of her marriage, but her heart was breaking."

"I wish that she had told me," said Harrison.

"She tried Harrison, but sometimes fate is not always on your side. She wrote you a letter, the last letter she ever wrote. She sealed it up, put a stamp on it and off we went to the post office. She was so happy. She had made a decision, and she knew it was the right one."

"I never did hear what happened to the trucker who swerved into the oncoming traffic. I just assumed he fell asleep. The next thing I knew the car was in the ditch and on fire. Two men dragged her out and then saved me. I only had scratches, but Elizabeth was paralyzed from the waist down. She spent the rest of her life in a wheelchair."

"Dear God, I thought she died in that accident."

"She lived the rest of her life in seclusion. I built a secret room for her and took care of her until she died two years ago."

Tears fell down Harrison's cheeks, his voice quivered. "Why?" he asked, his voice raspy with emotion.

"She didn't want to be a burden to you. She thought you could never love an invalid."

Bradley stepped back into the shadows. He stared at the old man lying in bed. It was painful to see the hurt in these cold, teary eyes. He stepped forward.

"I have something for you," he said holding out the letter.

Harrison glanced at it. "What is it?"

"The night of the wreck, just before the men pulled me from the burning car, I spotted it and grabbed onto it. I've had it ever since, waiting for this day. This is the letter...the last letter."

Harrison took it into his hands. It was still sealed, the address faded, but still visible. He held it to his cheek and closed his eyes. "I've prayed for so many years for one more chance to touch her," he said, his voice weak and fading, almost a whisper. He handed it back to Bradley. "Read it to me. Please."

Bradley carefully slit the flap on the envelope and slowly slid the brittle paper from its home. He unfolded the letter and began to read:

"My dearest Harrison,

How are you, my love? I was so happy to see you. I can't tell you how my heart felt. For a few fleeting moments it was not breaking, and then our meeting was over, and you went away."

"I remember how it was in the beginning. I loved you so much and we had so much fun. I hated when the day came to an end and it was time for sleep. I didn't want to be away from you even for a moment, and then you went off to war. I don't think a day went by that I didn't cry myself to sleep. The days seemed to drag by, days into weeks and weeks into months. But I never lost hope that you would come back to me. Every day I said a prayer for God to watch over you and bring you back to me. My heart aches again as I write this letter."

"I remember the day the letter from the War Department came. It was a beautiful summer day. I remember thinking how could anything go wrong on such a wonderful day. I knew it was bad news even before the postman handed me the letter. I could see it in his eyes. My life as I knew it came to an end on that summer day. I wanted to die. I couldn't imagine ever being happy again. You know I've always believed in God, even after the letter, but I never could understand how He could be so cruel. How could He have such things as hurricanes, tornadoes, and how could He give you to me and then take you away."

"I won't dwell on how I met Paul. It's not important, and it was the biggest mistake of my life. The only good thing I got out of the relationship was Rachael. I dearly love her, but I don't think I can take another minute living with Paul. The saddest part of it all is that I don't think I can be happy with any man, but you. I've never stopped loving you even when I thought you were dead. It didn't change a thing. I went right on loving you, still do today, as much as I did when we were together all those years ago."

"I write this letter to tell you that I'm leaving my husband. I can't take it anymore. I know he tries. In his own way, he loves me, but not the way I want to be loved. Maybe if I had never known you, I could have been satisfied with him, but I'm afraid he stands too deep in your shadow for me to ever be truly happy with him. Therefore, I am leaving him and would like to know if I could come home to you. I know a lot has happened. I'm married and have a child. I'll understand if you don't want me, but if you do, I promise I'll love you for the rest of my life. I know we will have many problems in the beginning, but we can work them out. As long as we're together, we can do anything."

"Either way, please let me know. I will be anxiously waiting for your reply. Whatever happens, remember I love you and will always love you no matter what."

Love always,
Elizabeth

With shaking hands, Bradley refolded the letter and slid it back into the envelope. He slowly handed it to Harrison. The old man took it and held it to his chest with both hands.

From his coat pocket, Bradley removed a small black box and handed it to Harrison. "I found this in the bottom of the box with your letters."

Harrison turned the key and opened it. He studied the contents for a moment and then with one hand he motioned for Spencer and Madison. Tears streamed down their faces as they came closer.

Harrison handed the box to Spencer. "This is the wedding ring I was going to put on Elizabeth's finger and never got the chance. Take it, son. Through you we can complete the circle."

"Thank you, Grandfather," said Spencer. "I'm so sorry for you."

"Oh, don't be sorry for me, son," he said. He then rolled over and stared into the darkened room. "My happiness is yet to be."

THE END

ABOUT THE AUTHOR

In 1966, Scott turned down a contract with the Detroit Tigers to pursue his lifelong dream of becoming a published author by earning a degree at Ohio University. In 1996 with a lifelong dream of being a writer, Scott started writing short stories. Within two years, he had four stories published. Since then, his first novel, *All Those Years Ago*, was published, *Summer Heat*, his fifth novel, was published in May 2012 and his bestseller, *The Mansfield Killings*, based on a true story, was published in October 2012. To date, Scott has published 16 novels.

The Mansfield Killings, The Killing Road, Summer Heat, Summer Harvest, Against the Wind and The Geezer Bench will soon be made into major motion pictures.

Now, Scott spends nearly all his time writing his next novel.

Scott lives in Mansfield, Ohio, where most of his novels take place, with his wife, Deb.

Visit his web site, www.scottcfields.com to learn more.

www.ingramcontent.com/pod-product-compliance
Lightning Source LLC
Chambersburg PA
CBHW060323260626
47160CB00007B/2659